WINTER'S PEAK

WINTER BLACK SERIES: SEASON TWO
BOOK FIVE

MARY STONE

Copyright © 2024 by Mary Stone Publishing

All rights reserved.

No part of this book may be reproduced in any form or by any electronic or mechanical means, including information storage and retrieval systems, without written permission from the author, except for the use of brief quotations in a book review.

❦ Created with Vellum

To all sexual harassment survivors: your strength, courage, and resilience inspire us all. This book is dedicated to your voices and your journey toward healing.

DESCRIPTION

It's lonely at the top. And deadly at the bottom.

Sexual harassment isn't the type of case Private Investigator Winter Black usually takes. But it's a welcome distraction from whoever's been sending creepy, anonymous text messages to her phone and set up cameras to spy on her home and office. And after her new client reveals that one of her female coworkers hanged herself after fending off their boss's sexual advances, Winter suspects there's more to the story.

When another woman disappears, she's certain.

Posing as an employee, Winter sets her sights on uncovering the truth at the climbing equipment company, starting with the powerful and well-connected boss who seems intent on showing her the ropes—in more ways than one. But when an employee's body is discovered at the bottom of a gorge, strangled by self-tightening rock-climbing knots, it's clear there's a killer on the loose, and he knows exactly what he's doing. And his victims aren't random.

With employees dropping like flies, Winter must uncover the madman behind the murders before she becomes the next victim caught in the killer's web.

The mystery and suspense continue with Winter's Peak, the fifth book in the Winter Black Season Two series, a gripping thriller that will tie you up in knots. If you give someone enough rope, they'll eventually hang themselves. Or you.

1

Inside a world of dark shapes and muffled sounds, Parker Roy tried to curl in on himself—an instinctive, protective action against some unseen predator. But thick ropes limited his movements, biting into his flesh with every small shift. His mind raced, each thought a mix of fear and confusion.

He woke up face down, bound and gagged in the back of some stranger's moving vehicle. His head throbbed, like coming out of anesthesia. The rough fabric in his mouth stifled his attempts to cry out, leaving him helplessly scanning his memory for clues as to how this happened.

All he remembered was clocking out of his work computer and heading toward his vehicle.

As he was inserting his keys to unlock his pickup, someone swooped in from behind, wrapping a rope around his neck. Parker thrashed, trying to scream. His assailant held on with the strength of a boa constrictor.

He remembered snippets of a man—definitely a guy dressed in black, a cloth mask covering his face—binding him. Goggles obscured his eyes, the anti-glare coating winking green in the dim light.

"Wrap the spool with the tag end…and…drive the knots to the bottom…" the man had mumbled to himself, narrating the deft movements of his gloved hands as he trussed Parker.

After that, Parker's vision brightened and went spotty, as if he'd been staring at the sun, and a cacophony of sound blared in his ears before everything turned to black. As he passed out, he'd been sure he was dying.

Sometime during the interminable drive, his consciousness came back into focus like candles being lit in a dark room one by one. Awareness of his body came next. Pain and pressure. A rope knot at the back of his neck, plus several down his spine, jabbing into his skin and vertebrae. His legs were lashed together and bent back behind him. More knots dug into the soles of his feet.

Every time the SUV bounced or took a fast curve, his body smacked into the hatch door. Wrapped tighter than a pork tenderloin, he jounced around in the back of vehicle, the knots tightening with every bump, leeching his limbs of blood.

He struggled to swallow. A wad of rope or nylon Paracord had been stuffed into his mouth. It prevented him from closing his jaw fully, so saliva drooled from the corner of his lips. The tears in his eyes brought about by the pain and the terror of his situation made his nose run.

He could barely breathe.

After what felt like forever, the SUV came to a stop.

Parker's eyes darted from side to side, but there was nothing to see through the back window save a few twinkling stars in a cool black sky. Blood rushed in his ears, his heart hammering. He listened as the driver stepped out, slamming the door behind him. Heavy footfalls crunched on rocks or gravel. Then the hatch flew open.

The man in the mask stood before him, looking down. Again, Parker tried to scream.

Who are you? Why are you doing this? Let me go! I'll give you anything!

The rope was so tight—the ball knot jabbing at the back of his throat—all that came out was a pathetic squeak.

Silhouetted by a crescent moon, the stranger grasped Parker by the ropes on his back and dragged him out of the SUV, dropping him on the ground. The impact pulled the ropes still tighter.

Parker was hitched to something—a slip line in the ties attached to something stationary. Every motion pulled against it, constricting, compressing.

When the stranger took a spool of Paracord and fixed it to a large carabiner on his hip, Parker knew the specialized kernmantle rope was no coincidence. This person was a rock climber.

Parker tried rolling over to see where the stranger had taken him. He smelled pine and dirt. Wilderness. Saw jagged rocks framed by fluffy trees. In any other scenario, a great place to climb. Maybe he'd even climbed here before. It was less than an hour out of town, possibly somewhere in El Barranco State Park.

Grabbing the rope near the back of Parker's neck where he'd tied in a fixed loop, the stranger dragged him down a narrow path. Parker's legs scraped on rocks and spiny plants. They were in the middle of nowhere, no one but the moon and stars to witness his plight.

Parker struggled. Each breath was harder to take. He couldn't feel his fingers anymore, his feet. He was so cold.

The man dragging him was neither huge nor small, his physique perfectly average, at least as far as Parker could see. But he was strong, never once faltering as he walked.

Finally, the masked man threw Parker against the trunk of a tree. He snatched a knife from a pack on his back and, in one swift and clumsy motion, cut the binds from around Parker's mouth.

The blade scraped across Parker's skin, splitting his lips.

"Scream if you want to." The stranger's voice was low, gravelly, and cold, intentionally terrifying. "No one can hear you."

"Please, please, let me go!" Parker blubbered, blood and snot pouring down his face and neck, spattering the earth below him. "What did I ever do to you?"

The stranger stood absolutely still, his stance wide as he gazed down. "You did nothing, that's what you did." He wrapped his hand around the nylon line leading from his belt to Parker's binds. "Wrap the spool with the tag end. Overhand, use the standing."

What's with the fucking commentary?! Parker felt like he was trapped in some kind of YouTube tutorial for serial killers.

"Please." Parker's eyes darted, desperately watching those quick hands go to work on yet another knot. "I don't understand what you mean! I never hurt anybody!"

"Second knot to the tag. Pull the standing tight." The stranger took the loop he'd made and placed it over Parker's neck.

"You're crazy!" Parker threw his weight back, trying to pull away, as the stranger's hand tightened on the rope.

"Drive the knots to the bottom." He yanked hard. The loop he'd made snatched tight, cutting off Parker's final breath.

Parker squirmed and struggled, knots driving deep enough to snap his bones. The creak of the rope shrieked in his ears.

The last thing Parker saw were those green lenses, hovering in front of his face. The stranger watched him suffer until the nighttime breeze stilled and the stars in the inky sky faded…and he was gone.

2

Winter Black drummed her fingers on the plastic lid of her mocha latte as the woman on the other end of her phone droned on. The case was done—a simple matter of tracking down a thieving ex-employee so he could be served with papers. All and all, she'd worked on it for about two hours, mainly listening to her client talk more than actually providing any services.

Tact had never been Winter's strong suit. If not for the matter of collecting the second half of her fee, she would've just cut the woman off and ended the call.

"By the Lord God, I can't thank you enough, Ms. Black," Minnie said. "Why, Everett used to be such a good employee. You never can know just who you can trust…"

"Ain't that the truth." Sitting behind her desk, Winter caught sight of an SXSW poster on one office wall—an orange cow on a yellow background kicking its hind legs in the air. The cow had a conspiratorial look on its face, like it wanted to start a fire. Winter had found it when she'd gone thrifting with her gramma for decorations for her new office. She still wasn't sure if she loved it or hated it. It made her feel something. That was all she knew for sure.

Sighing, she let her focus continue past the other posters —the Austin Crawfish Festival, the Oyster Festival. The first annual Squirrel Fest, her favorite.

Through the interior window that gave her a view of the entire office, Winter spotted her assistant. Where Ariel sat at her desk in the front area, her long, curly brown hair hung loose, bouncing a little with each enthusiastic keyboard stroke.

Winter smiled. Moments like this were precisely why she had an assistant.

"You are so welcome," Winter cut off the chatty old woman. "I'm afraid I have another client meeting. My assistant will help you get everything wrapped up."

"But—"

Winter transferred the call and yelled, "I need you to collect my fee from line two."

"You got it!" Ariel tossed a bright smile over her shoulder. That young woman was a bundle of untapped energy, always ready and willing to take on anything Winter threw her way.

Good luck, girl.

As she turned back to the open laptop on the desk before her, Winter caught sight of the front door opening in her periphery.

A woman stepped inside, her brown ponytail wet from the spring drizzle outside. Her brightly made-up eyes scanned the office. She was dressed in a tight white t-shirt and high-waisted khaki cargo pants with hiking boots. With her long eyelashes, thick lips, and huge boobs, she would've made a good Lara Croft in the inevitable *Tomb Raider* remake.

Rising from her desk, Winter stepped through her door

into the lobby. Poor Ariel was still trying to get a word in edgewise on the phone.

"Good morning." Winter smiled, leaning against the doorframe.

"Are you Winter Black?" The newcomer's voice was soft and quiet, even a little shaky. Her deerlike eyes flashed to Winter's face, then down to the floor as she gently poked at the floor with a boot.

"I am. How can I help you?"

"I want to hire you. I, uh…" She was wringing her hands together, eyes darting. Nervous about something, maybe even afraid. Like so many people who found themselves in need of Winter's services. "I need your help."

"Come into my office." Winter held open the door for the woman and gestured to a worn leather chair across from her desk. She snatched up her lukewarm mocha latte and took a sip before settling into her own rolling seat. After opening a blank case file on her laptop, she poised her fingers over the keys. "Can I have your name, please?"

"Helen. Helen Marchand. I want to hire you to look into my employer. You would keep that confidential, right?"

"Absolutely. Who's your employer?"

"I work for Cumberland. It's an outdoor equipment company with a focus on mountain climbing."

Winter typed the name into her intake form, then copied and pasted for a quick Google search. "Cumberland Mountain Climbing Equipment, LLC. They sell mostly in bulk to retail stores like Sierra, but also have an online shop and a few storefronts of their own. Publicly traded, their CEO is—"

"Nathan Lynch. He's my boss. He's the one I want to look into." Helen crossed her legs. Her hands kept wringing, skin turning white with the pressure.

"What do you suspect him of?"

"I don't *suspect* him of anything. I *know*. Sexual harassment."

Winter raised an eyebrow, lifting her hands off the keyboard. "Oh?"

"It's not just me. It's every woman in the company. He treats the office like his own private nightclub. I tried going to HR, but the hiring manager doesn't care. He's just Nathan's crony. I don't know what to do. It's not about me. I can handle it. It's just—"

"Ms. Marchand, I—"

"Please, call me Helen."

Winter bobbed her chin. "Helen, then. What would you ideally want to get out of hiring me?"

"I want Nathan to get what he deserves. He should be fired, arrested, and on the sex offender registry."

That wasn't the answer Winter had expected. "Sexual harassment is usually a civil matter. Have you tried talking to a lawyer?"

"I don't want money." She shook her head hard. "Besides, there's no point until I have proof. I talked to another P.I., and he told me to try hiding a camera at my desk. I have footage of Nathan making all kinds of sick comments to girls in the office, harassing them. Telling them how to dress."

That sat in Winter's stomach like rotten milk. Still, she had to be realistic. "None of that is necessarily criminal behavior. No matter how disgusting they are, words are still a civil matter. Unless you suspect he's been doing something worse…?" Winter trailed off, hoping the woman would know what she meant.

Ariel had finished with her call and drifted toward Winter's open door. She slid into a chair in the corner of the office, her big, brown eyes studying Helen. In her right arm, she cradled her trusty iPad as she typed out notes with her left hand.

Helen took a deep breath and sighed. "Yes. I think he did."

The rotten feeling in Winter's gut twisted sharply. She waited patiently for Helen to continue, a leftover habit from her time in the FBI. Whether she was talking to a perpetrator, a witness, or a victim, she found most people were so uncomfortable with silence that she often got more out of them by saying nothing than by rattling off a dozen questions.

"There was a new employee. Christina Norris. Really sweet little thing. She had a side business teaching young kids how to climb. She was in her twenties." Helen sniffled and discreetly wiped a tear from the corner of her eye. "I think Nathan did something to her."

A throbbing anger pulsed to life at the back of Winter's brain. "What makes you think that?"

"Christina…" Her voice choked. She cleared her throat and swallowed hard. "She quit about two weeks ago. No explanation. Didn't even tell her boyfriend why. And then, last weekend, they found her. She'd hung herself a few days after quitting." She shivered out a quavering sigh. "And I think it's Nathan's fault."

The red-hot flame in Winter began to flicker, burning her insides like coal. "Ariel, bring Helen the new-client paperwork."

Helen straightened. "Does that mean you'll help me?"

Winter nodded. "If your boss is assaulting his employees, I'll find proof of it. I guarantee it."

"Thank you. I just…thank you." Helen pulled her phone from her purse and checked it before rising from her seat. "I should go."

Ariel approached and handed her a white folder. "This has all the official docs, as well as a lists of FAQs. If you'd rather do the paperwork online, there's a QR code in there."

"Thank you." Helen flashed Ariel a smile, then Winter, but

her face held no joy. She headed back outside into the cloudy day, her shoulders hunched as she scurried to her car.

With her eyes narrowed, Winter watched Helen through the glass wall that faced the street. The woman kept checking over her shoulder, as if she thought somebody might be following her. How much had she risked by coming to the office?

Ariel stepped up beside her, hugging her iPad to her chest. "I'll get started looking into Nathan Lynch's history."

"Don't forget to look into Helen too." Winter went back into her office. She couldn't officially get started until Helen returned the contract with her retainer fee, but her brain was already turning on the case.

It was difficult to imagine a young woman taking her life over a few untoward comments or wandering hands. But maybe there was more to the story.

3

Special Agent Noah Dalton sat in his Supervisory Special Agent's office waiting for the man to arrive and begin the meeting he'd set up. This was a power move on his boss's part, Noah had concluded. Weston Falkner was making him wait for no other reason than he could. Clearly, the SSA felt Noah needed to be reminded who was in charge around here. And maybe that was fair.

That didn't make it any less irritating.

Noah had never been especially good at following orders. Whether during his time in the Marines or while working with the VCU in Richmond, Noah used standard procedure more as a guideline than a strict directive. Action was what really mattered—following his instincts and getting the job done—while never disobeying direct commands.

Well, maybe not *never*.

In the past, as long as he kept bringing in results, his superiors had been willing to look the other way concerning the occasional overstepping of bounds or failure to follow indirect orders.

Falkner was different. Though Noah had at first assessed

him as being pretty much exactly like his old SSA down in Richmond—a kind of Aiden Parrish 2.0—he was starting to see the error of this simplistic logic.

From the moment Noah transferred to Austin, Falkner had been riding his ass. The first time they met, the man had looked right through him with a curl to his lip like assessing the damage of a car crash. He constantly questioned Noah's devotion to the job, his ability to follow procedure, and whether he was even cut out to be in the FBI—or so it always seemed.

Noah bristled just thinking of it. He wasn't a rookie who needed to be put through his paces before proving himself to the Bureau. He was an old hat, serving with distinction in Richmond for years before making the move to Texas.

But Noah couldn't sneeze without Falkner questioning if he was doing it right.

Maybe by thinking of Falkner as just another Aiden Parrish—who'd seemed like a gargoyle at first—Noah had secretly been hoping one day that rough exterior would crack.

The office door finally opened, and SSA Falkner stepped in.

He was only a year from retirement, but other than a face weathered like an ex-U.S. president, the fifty five year old showed no signs of age. His back was straight, his body wiry with muscle. Though his buzzed hair was white, he had a full head of it. And his eyes were as shrewd and sharp as icicles.

Falkner said nothing as he walked to his side of the desk and sat in his leather chair. He took up a few documents, filed them into manila folders on his desk, and put those away in a nearby metal cabinet before lifting his cold gaze. "Agent Dalton. I assume you know why I wanted to speak to you."

Noah wasn't sure if he was expected to answer that or if Falkner just wanted him to avert his eyes like a scolded child.

A wanted killer had kidnapped Winter's contractor, Kline Hurst, and taken him to an isolated farm, where she'd had every intention of doing to him what she'd done to her other victims. Namely, stabbing him in the heart.

Falkner had explicitly ordered Noah to stay away from the case. But Winter needed him and, together, they'd taken down the perpetrator and rescued Kline. The case was closed, the killer stopped. And Noah had left the scene before the local PD showed up.

He'd known he'd get in trouble for what he'd done. In light of that, he supposed it was a bit fair if Falkner treated him like a naughty child.

"I had no choice. I'm a cop, first and foremost. I might not wear blue, but serving and protecting is in my job description. Fidelity, bravery, integrity. I'm not going to leave anyone to face off with a killer on their own. Not when I can help."

Falkner's eyes narrowed into slits. "Not when it's your wife."

Noah kept his lips closed so Falkner wouldn't see him clenching his teeth. They stared at one another, neither blinking. Like a couple of lions gearing up for a fight.

Falkner broke eye contact first when he sighed and looked down at his desk. "I'm placing you on probationary leave."

"What?" Noah slapped the arm of his chair. "That's bull!"

"Is it?" Falkner tented his long, thick-knuckled fingers and looked at Noah from over them. "You've made it very clear where your loyalty lies, and it is not with the department."

Noah's heart pounded in his ears. The truth was, he wasn't exactly shocked by this development. But that didn't mean he was any less upset. "Would you ask another agent to let his wife go alone into a situation with a known killer?"

"The Bureau asks everything from their agents. It asks them to keep secrets from their families, work long hours, repeatedly risk their lives, and suffer through trauma that would break lesser men and women."

"That didn't answer my question."

Falkner stood and paced to the window, his back straight and taut. "I don't know how things worked in Richmond, but the Austin Violent Crime Unit is not the Noah and Winter Show. If I can't count on you to follow orders, I can't count on you at all. And that means that no matter how talented an investigator you might be, you are a liability."

Noah clenched a fist and rose to his feet. He was taller than Falkner, with broader shoulders, and had a good fifty pounds on him. But none of that mattered here. If anything, it made him feel more helpless.

"I'm devoted to my work. I'm willing to do everything necessary—"

"Everything? Even if it means leaving your wife to handle her own problems?"

A tension headache began to pulse through Noah's skull from all the jaw-clenching. Try as he might, he couldn't force himself to answer that.

"I'm putting you on probationary leave for three weeks. And when you come back, I'll be expecting a full recommitment to the FBI and everything that entails. Or I'll be accepting your resignation."

There was nothing more to say, and certainly no way to change Falkner's mind. No squeezing blood from that stone.

Noah crossed the hall into his little closet of an office and began to gather his things. The front of his desk was pressed against his partner's so that they faced each other. There was no window in this room, no access to outside air or light.

This must be what suffocation feels like.

The FBI was his life, everything that mattered to him. Or at least, it had been before he fell in love with a dark-haired, trouble-making angel called Winter Black. He couldn't lose either of them. He didn't know who he was without both. Besides, ever since Winter had gone into the private sector, she'd relied on Noah and his access to FBI resources to help her with her work.

An old twinge niggled at his heart, a memory of losing Winter and the feeling of total helplessness that always came with it. Noah tried his best not to think about when Winter was kidnapped by her sick younger brother. How he'd been left reeling, begging God for a way to help the woman he loved. Not knowing what was happening to her.

Once he had her back in his arms, he'd promised himself he'd never let her out of his sight again. That he'd always protect her, no matter the consequences.

If he lost the FBI, how would he be able to take care of Winter? His hands twinged with tiny, electric zaps, reminding him he was only made of flesh and bone. Just like Winter.

The illusion of his own invincibility had faded along with his twenties, coinciding vaguely with his first tour of duty where he watched one invincible person after another get taken down. Now Noah knew exactly how easy it was to die. And neither he nor anybody he loved was exempt from it.

With a final, longing glance at the two pathetically unrealistic plastic bamboo plants, Pokey and his brand-new "gal pal," Pokette, Noah left his office and walked out of the building. As he climbed into Beulah—his red Ford F-350—he dug his phone from his pocket and called his wife.

He wasn't sure what he'd tell her. A part of him wanted to keep the whole thing secret. Lord knew, Winter had enough to worry about without him bringing her down with his drama. At the same time, the idea of lying to her was like a searing hot poker in his gut.

"Hey, baby." Her sweet voice came on the line, quenching the painful heat in his soul like water to a man dying of thirst. "How you doing?"

"I'm all right." Noah cringed even at that little lie. "How's your mornin', darlin'?"

"I have a new case and a feeling it's going to take a lot of my time and energy."

"Oh, yeah? What's it about?"

"White-collar CEO type who may or may not be sexually assaulting his employees."

Noah wished that proposition shocked him, but he'd lost his innocence about such things a long time ago.

"I haven't *officially* taken it on yet," Winter continued. "I wanted to talk to you before I decided."

Well, there was a first. "Really? Why?"

"Because we haven't had much time to just be together lately. And I know we promised we'd make more time for each other."

Noah smiled gently. "That's what I get for marrying a superhero. You gotta do what you gotta do. I'm behind you a hundred percent. You know that."

And so does my boss.

"I do." She laughed softly.

"Actually, I'm gonna have some time off this next little while. I'll be able to work around your schedule."

"Why? What's wrong?"

"Well…" Noah rubbed the back of his neck, chewing on his words before spitting them out. "Falkner gave me a bit of time off to think about what I've done."

"He put you on leave?" She sounded worried.

"I promise you, it's no big thing. Paid leave is pretty standard after going through a nasty situation."

That wasn't a lie.

"After what happened with your last case…what I did and then didn't stick around to explain…he just thought I might need a bit of time off to recalibrate, is all."

That wasn't a lie either. So why did Noah feel so slimy?

"Okay…" Winter didn't sound convinced. "You headed home now?"

"Yeah. I was gonna go peek in on Kline. See how he's healing up."

Winter's biological father had been staying in their guest room since his ordeal at the farm.

"Have you gotten any more information about his background?" Noah didn't like the interrogatory tone that entered his voice, but he couldn't help it.

So far, Kline Hurst—aka John Drewitt, aka the long-lost one-night stand who'd helped bring Winter into existence—had been an exemplary house guest.

But Noah still didn't trust him as far as he could spit. Why hadn't Kline told Winter the truth? Why not just be straight with her? With him? He'd lied to get close to Winter, even using a false name, and that did not sit well with Noah.

"We're working on it. I'd like to have him come back and finish up the work he started in the office," Winter said. "Will you let him know that?"

"Sure thing." Noah cracked his knuckles. Mention of Kline bothered him for more than one reason. Not long after learning who Kline really was, Winter had gotten a text from an untraceable number.

Give your Daddy a kiss from me.

That plus the closed-circuit camera she'd found at her gramma and grampa's house had Noah tossing and turning all night long. And he felt compelled to do everything to protect her.

"Are you there?" Winter's cool voice brushed over him, pulling him back into the moment.

"I'm here." He flashed a smile to keep his tone smooth. "You go ahead and get on your case, darlin'. I can already hear that old excitement in your voice."

"Do you think I'm crazy?"

Noah chuckled. "Imma need more context for that question, please."

"I hear the most hideous stories, work on the sickest of problems, yet you say I sound excited."

"You're excited to help. You have passion for your job." Noah pulled the phone away from his mouth so she wouldn't hear him sigh. He remembered a time when he'd shared that passion. Lately, all his FBI duties had felt like a distraction from what he really cared about. "I love that about you." He wished he were saying that to her face so she could see the sincerity in his eyes. "I've always loved that about you."

"I love you too." Her words filled him up, steadying his hands. "Talk to you soon, baby."

4

Winter hung up, but the conversation lingered like fruit flies buzzing around her brain. There was something off about the way Noah sounded.

She didn't blame him. He was always protective. Winter herself was still wrapping her head around the information Kline had given her.

Kline. She couldn't think of him any other way. The word *father* didn't feel right, the sound striking her ear like an out-of-tune piano. She'd known the man who raised her wasn't her father for a long time, ever since discovering one of her mother's old journals lamenting that she didn't know how to find "John," a man she'd met at a club. But that hadn't mattered, because the man who chose to raise her loved her like his own.

In the hospital after his attack, Kline verified her mother's story. *"I met your mother at some club. I've forgotten the name. She attended the local college and was there for a social mixer put on by her sorority. I was just passing through before traveling back to Texas. I remember your mom was there with another guy, and they got into a big fight. She ran out of the club, and I wanted to make sure she was okay."* He wiped his eye with his good hand. *"We hit it off and ended up in a hotel room. When I woke up the next morning, she was gone."*

He wouldn't give her details about when or why he changed his name, though.

"I'll save that story for another day. But I'm John. John Drewitt."

Winter rubbed her eyes. She knew she needed to dig further into Kline Hurst. Or rather, John Drewitt. Noah was going to insist. But she didn't have much time to think on it before Ariel walked into her office.

"Hey. Is there anything else you needed before I head out?"

Winter's hands dropped away from her eyes as she pushed aside her concern about Noah. "Did you get anything on our new client?"

"Helen Marchand seems perfectly legit. Nothing much to say about her. Unfortunately, the same is kind of true of her boss." Ariel pulled on her pale-blue raincoat. "I sent everything to your inbox."

"Great." Winter turned to her computer and typed in the passcode to open the screen. "Have a good night."

As Ariel faded from the office and into the drizzly street, Winter read the background she'd put together for Nathan Lynch.

Graduating with an MBA at age twenty-four from Vanderbilt—his father's alma mater where he pulled mostly gentlemen's Cs—Lynch first worked for his father's investment firm. Soon, he left Daddy's company and bounced around, first landing a CFO position at a sporting goods company called Carmean Sports before becoming CEO at thirty-one. After just two years, Lynch sold all his holdings and cut ties with Carmean. Then he disappeared for a long time.

Winter hadn't yet gotten to the part when he started work with Cumberland when the office phone began to ring. Not looking up from the computer screen, Winter picked up the receiver. "Black Investigations."

"Hello. Might I speak with Winter?"

The voice was unfamiliar, quiet, and a bit nervous, with a pale Southern lilt à la Dolly Parton.

"Speaking."

"Oh, hello. Um, my name is Opal Drewitt. I'm your aunt."

Drewitt.

This wasn't the first time Winter had heard the name Opal either. At the hospital, during Kline's initial evaluation after his attack, she'd finally gotten around to asking Kline how he'd found her in the first place.

"A few months back, my sister, Opal, reached out and told me about how she'd submitted her blood to one of them DNA testing sites. Well, a match came back, saying she had a close relative...a niece. You see, Opal's my only sibling. I don't have any other family. She put two and two together and knew exactly who the child must belong to. Me."

That seemed an easy enough story.

The only problem was Winter had never submitted her DNA to any such site.

So who did?

Opal told Kline she'd messaged Winter's profile on the site and gotten a return message from a so-called *friend* of hers who had apparently taken her DNA covertly and submitted it to the site.

Terrible invasion of privacy didn't even begin to cover it. Somebody had stolen Winter's DNA, put it on the internet, and orchestrated her reconnecting with estranged family members—all without her knowledge or permission. But why would anybody want to do such a thing?

And who?

Justin? It couldn't be. Her brother was locked in solitary at ADX Valdez, a supermax prison at an undisclosed location in the Chihuahuan Desert of New Mexico. He would never get out.

Painful little goose bumps grew on Winter's arms and legs—a warning from her gut that something wasn't right.

"Hello?" Opal said.

"I'm here." She clenched and unclenched her fist, centering herself. "I've been wondering if you might contact me."

"Your father…I mean, my brother…said it'd be okay. Is it?"

"Sure, Opal, yes." Winter wasn't one hundred percent sure it *was* okay, but it seemed like the prudent thing to do was keep all these new relatives talking.

"Thank you for all you're doing for Kline. That was quite the scare."

"It was. And then quite the surprise with his…confession."

"About being your father?" Opal coughed. "I can only imagine, dear."

"Yes, about being my father. What other skeletons does he have in his closet?"

"Oh, just that!" The woman let out a tiny nervous laugh that didn't go unnoticed.

But Winter was currently more interested in the DNA site than Kline and his secrets. Those had been kept for years now—they could keep a little longer. There were more immediate threats. "Let me ask you something. I understand somebody else was running my account on the DNA site. Could you tell me their name?"

"PJ. He says he misses you. He's your cousin. Is that right?"

"I don't have a cousin named PJ." Winter's voice sounded

flat despite the uncomfortable thrashing of her heart. "I don't know a man or woman or anyone called PJ at all."

Give your Daddy a kiss from me.

The words from the mystery text twisted through her brain, again and again.

"I need you to do something for me, Opal." The woman's name felt strange in Winter's mouth.

"Of course, dear. You name it."

"If PJ contacts you again, I need you to call me right away. I mean it. Whoever they are, they didn't do this to do any of us any favors." Winter looked up at the rain-spattered window again. No one was there, the streets empty. Still, she couldn't shake the feeling that someone was watching her every move. "I think we all might be in serious danger."

5

Aliyah Andry sighed as she finished organizing the receipts from her newest client. After another long day at Marburg Accounting, she was ready to pack up and head home. As she glanced at the time on her computer, she noticed it was already past closing. Her new place of work had emptied out, with nothing but the hum of the water cooler to keep her company.

As she tapped away at her keyboard, finalizing the last details of her ever-expanding spreadsheet, Aliyah's thoughts began to wander into dark corners she tried so hard to stay out of. Christina's face surfaced in her mind, and Aliyah shuddered, haunted by what her friend had done to herself.

With a heavy heart, Aliyah went through the motions of checking all the windows, ensuring they were securely locked. Then, lugging her computer bag and oversize purse onto her shoulder, she headed toward the door.

She'd tried calling Christina's boyfriend to check in on him, but Bryan wasn't answering. She could only imagine what he must be going through.

In the days leading up to her suicide, Christina had

withdrawn from everyone, according to her former Cumberland coworker, Helen. Aliyah had tried calling Christina after she quit there, but she never drove over to knock on the door.

Now it was too late.

Guilt weighed on Aliyah's shoulders like a wet blanket. She'd done wrong by her friend.

When Christina and Bryan were laid off from Get Your Climb On, Aliyah had already been working for Cumberland for more than a year and had encouraged her friends to apply. The pay was good, the benefits package unbeatable, and the company was expanding with employee share options. There was not a more lucrative job in the industry. The only caveat was her sleazy boss Nathan Lynch. All the women employees learned to just put up with him.

But she imagined Nathan had done more than simply harass Christina. Like the wolf he was, the CEO of Cumberland liked to corner the most vulnerable of the flock, and Christina was a sweetheart.

Still, she'd had Bryan working alongside her. Surely, her boyfriend could've protected her. That was his job, not Aliyah's…

Rationalizing her inaction only succeeded in making Aliyah feel sick. She'd left Cumberland a month ago for a boring but stress-free job with an accounting firm. She'd escaped Nathan while leaving Christina behind. Pressing her back against the wall beside the alarm box at the front door, she took slow, deep breaths.

Aliyah wanted nothing more than to claim ignorance over what had happened, but that was bullshit. She'd told herself Nathan really wasn't that bad. But if that were true, why had she taken a pay cut just to get away from him?

Why hadn't she warned Christina?

Even Aliyah's new employers had given her a pass when

they noticed that little blip on her résumé, the mention of Nathan Lynch's name as a reference.

The Marburg sisters—and everybody else in Austin—seemed to know exactly what kind of man he was. A powerful and well-connected one who the court system couldn't seem to touch, no matter how many lives he shattered.

Aliyah clenched a fist around her lanyard as she headed to her SUV. It wasn't her responsibility to warn Christina. She'd worked at Cumberland for months by the time Aliyah left. She was a big girl. She should've known too.

Then again, Christina was so sheltered, innocent. Homeschooled. Churchgoing. She'd never stood a chance against Nathan Lynch.

Aliyah never should've suggested she apply to Cumberland in the first place.

Bitter tears welled in Aliyah's eyes, and grief tore through her body as she reached the parking lot.

Since Christina's death, Aliyah couldn't seem to stop herself from crying. During the day, she kept herself busy with work. At night, she kept herself drunk to keep from feeling the pain.

A bottle of red wine called to her from home, promising another numb, dreamless night.

6

By now, I should've learned to never trust anyone. When I first met Aliyah, I should've known better. I should've seen behind her sweet, open nature to the cold creature underneath. But I believed her. Trusted her.

I waited in my Jeep at the far corner of the parking lot that adjoined Marburg Accounting. Everybody else had gone home for the day. One thing I knew about Aliyah was that she liked to work late. At Cumberland, she had a hard time getting her ass out of bed and getting into work on time, but she'd made up for it by staying late in the evenings.

Aliyah always skirted the rules. With her tight coils of black hair, her big brown eyes, and every inch of her dark skin so perfect without a blemish or visible pore, she could get away with anything, and she knew it.

And Aliyah—dragging Christina into Cumberland. Christina...
You were special and delicate and so very beautiful.
And now, you're gone.
Withered like a flower in a basement, dying a lonely death. It

was Aliyah who so mishandled you. She broke you. And that pathetic little man you let touch you.

I'm going to make it better. I promise.

The place where Aliyah was going, where Parker was, used to be my sanctum.

I brought you there once straight from work. We called it a field trip. You climbed with me up the sheer cliff face and sat with me at the very top. We watched the sunset together.

The place was without magic now and devoid of peace, nothing more than a graveyard.

And I will fill it with the carcasses of every single person who conspired to keep us apart.

I'd watched Aliyah move behind the venetian blinds as she locked up the office for the evening. She'd be at her vehicle any second now.

Lucky for me, she drove a huge SUV with plenty of room for a guy my size to hide behind. I stepped out of my Jeep and crouched behind her SUV's rear bumper.

My heart beat faster. I recognized it as a rush of vertigo. A sensation I felt all the time on the ropes. The threat of death, always followed by the unstoppable rush every time you cheated it.

I learned to enjoy vertigo. Closing my eyes, I let the dizziness rush over me. I wasn't about to die. She was. But I was still risking every part of my life in this moment.

For you.

My senses sharpened. I heard the clip-clop of her short steps in those heels she liked to wear.

Parker had been the first person to experience my own take on the ancient art of binding, one that included several hard anchors and slipknots that slid forward but not back. Watching it work on him—the ropes strangling him to death the more he struggled—was a rush. I wanted to leave him to kill himself with the binds, but I noticed some flaws in my design, extra knots and missing lashings that prevented my elaborate net from tightening enough to finish the job.

Aliyah would get the upgraded version.

Ever since you died, I've been fantasizing about watching all your so-called friends strangle themselves to death in my ropes. Ripping apart their own flesh on the harsh fibers—like rabbits caught in a fence.

Aliyah stepped to her door and clicked it open without hopping in. She was rummaging around in her giant purse.

I tightened the thick bend of nylon kernmantle rope between my hands. I'd spent last night weaving together a two-foot-long, braided garrote. The thicker the rope, the more easily I could apply enough pressure to knock a person out without killing them.

When I surged forward, my pulse raced as I dropped the rope around her neck. Each tug sent a jolt of dark pleasure coursing through me, an intoxicating rush flooding each part of my body.

She released her keys and tried to scream. Her legs kicked, and her long acrylic nails clawed at my hands, but only for a moment.

I held her close, my muscles shaking. Not with fatigue, but with anticipation of what would come next. Just as she passed out, I released the pressure on her neck. I didn't want to kill her.

Not yet.

She mumbled and twitched as I threw her over my shoulder. The sleeper effect would only last a minute or two, but that was plenty of time to load her into the back of my Jeep.

I took the working end of a spool of bright-green rope—twin rope, a little thinner, a little more delicate. It took the knots more easily than the kernmantle.

First, her wrists, a standard parallel lashing. "Pass the

bight clockwise, reverse tension, over and again. A total of five. Cross one last time, out of sight and in-between. Pull it tight, so tight. She won't get out."

Below me, Aliyah was starting to come to.

She blinked and moaned and then finally looked at me and began to struggle. Just as she opened her mouth to scream, I flashed her my knife. That shut her up.

"Hold still," I said in a deeper, raspier voice. She had no idea who I was. It was clear in her wild, round eyes.

"Please let me go." Tears streamed down her cheeks, but she wasn't thrashing anymore. "Please don't hurt me…"

I tied off the lashing of her wrists tight enough that she squealed. Then I inched down her body and did the same work on her ankles. I didn't cut the rope but left some slack. I'd need it later as the mainline for a series of hitches running down her back.

"Hold still," I said again.

She followed orders. I had a feeling she'd be good at that.

As I worked the knot, I continued to speak to myself. "Pass the bight clockwise, reverse tension. Double cross, out of sight and in-between." I passed the rope between her legs, my hand tightening between the smooth skin of her thighs. She felt so warm, the blood rushing so hard under her flawless skin.

Her shirt had fallen open, and in her flailing, she'd ripped two buttons on her shirt. I could see the lace on her black bra.

"Oh, god…" The pathetic sob of her voice pulled me back into myself. "I'll do whatever you want. Just don't kill me."

"Of course you will." I recoiled my hand and slapped her across the face as hard as I could. "I know what you're trying to do. And it won't work on me." I yanked the rope as hard as I could. "Pull it tight, so tight."

Her moaning rained over me.

"Shut up!"

After tying the ends off in a square knot, I flipped her over and shoved her face against the floor of the Jeep. Then I trailed the rope up her back and tied her wrists to her ankles.

"Please don't kill me! Please!" She started to thrash again. As pathetic and pointless as it was, her movements made it harder to tie secure knots.

I snatched her chin in my hand. Jerking her head back, I wrapped a loose line in her mouth, cinching it tight, like a makeshift bridle for a horse. Then I tied that to her wrists and ankles.

Her eyes begged for mercy. I gave her some. Why the hell not. "Hold still and be quiet. The more you struggle, the quicker you'll die."

Just as I expected, she obeyed.

7

The next day, the strange conversation with Opal Drewitt lingered in Winter's brain. She'd gone into the office like any other morning, but after only an hour there, she couldn't shake the hopeless, wild desperation raging in her heart.

She had to get out.

With the rain letting up, she walked down sparkling streets and got a fresh mocha at the nearby coffeehouse. On her way back, a rainbow arched across the sky. She paused to stare at it, her mind simmering with confusion.

If her biological father had come into her life only a few years ago, she might've been ecstatic to meet him. And his sister—a whole new family. Not that anyone could replace the one she'd lost.

But after everything—after her brother kidnapped her, drugged her, exploited her, forced her to do horrible things that haunted her every night—it was hard to feel anything other than exhaustion and dread.

Her heart felt like it wasn't working properly. Apathy was the wrong emotion here. But how could she fix it?

Back at the office, Winter walked in on Ariel jabbing at her iPad and swearing like it owed her money. She smiled and kept her eyes down as she hung up her jacket. "Don't mind me."

"Nathan frickin' Lynch is trash." Ariel balled her fists.

"Oh, yeah?" One thing Winter liked about Ariel, when she had something to say, she left no room for ambiguity. "What makes you so sure?"

"Have you looked at him yet?"

Winter shook her head.

Ariel tapped at her screen, then flipped it around for her to see. A picture stared back at her of a classically handsome man in his early forties with a strong chin, bright-brown eyes, thick hair, and an incredibly muscular build. Not a bodybuilder type, but more like a chiseled Roman statue, the angles of which were practically visible under his tailored suit.

Winter searched for more in his confident, half-cocked smile, but there was nothing deeper to be read. "That's Nathan Lynch?"

"Doesn't he just look like the most arrogant dick you've ever met?"

Winter choked on her latte, some of it escaping her mouth in a sputtering spray. "I don't know. I've met a lot of arrogant dicks." She turned her head side to side, examining him from different angles. "You shouldn't make such strong assumptions at the very beginning of a case. It'll cloud your judgment."

Arial snorted.

Taking up a tissue, Winter dabbed at the little brown dots of coffee on her shirt. "You find anything in his background?"

"No. I'm still going through civil records, though. I have a feeling."

"Let me know what you find." Winter flashed a smile, then stepped past Ariel into her segregated little office. Setting down her cup, she noticed a voicemail on her office phone—a missed call from Helen just two minutes ago. She dropped into her chair and called her back, her knee bouncing up and down as she dialed.

"Hello?" The shaken tone in her voice immediately put Winter on edge.

"Helen? Is everything okay?"

"The police were just here. Aliyah is missing."

Winter sat forward in her chair. "Who's Aliyah?"

"Aliyah Andry. She used to work here, at Cumberland. She was the one who referred Christina."

"Used to? She left the company?"

"About a month ago."

"Why?"

Helen didn't answer right away. Her breath on the end of the line sounded a bit ragged.

"They found her car outside of her new office. The door was unlocked, and they found her keys on the ground."

Winter's stomach dropped. Leaving behind her keys was a very bad sign.

Still, before letting her mind run loose on that, she wanted an answer to her question. "Helen, why did Aliyah leave Cumberland?"

"You know why, don't you?" Helen's voice was so soft, gentle even. "I mean, I'm sure being in the FBI and then a private investigator, you've had to deal with your fair share of boys' clubs. It can wear you down after a while."

Winter hated how easy it was for her to relate to that. Though she supposed it was easy for just about any woman.

"I'm sorry, Winter. But I don't think I can go ahead with the investigation. I don't know why I came to talk to you in the first place…"

"Yes, you do."

"I think I need to call the whole thing off, okay? I don't want to end up…I mean…"

Winter pressed her palm flat on her desk. "You're scared. I understand. Given what you've been dealing with, I know how hard it had to be to come talk to me."

"What can you really do, right? All that's going to happen is I'll get in trouble, and then Nathan—"

"Do you think Nathan might've hurt Aliyah? Is he capable of that?" Winter asked the question, although she knew full well that normal, compassionate people often greatly underestimated what others were capable of.

"What if Aliyah left Cumberland and filed a suit against Nathan? What if…" Helen sniffled. "I don't know."

Not a great answer.

Winter drummed her fingers. Getting the information out of Helen was going to be difficult, and Winter couldn't just mosey into the company to question employees outright, not when it was the boss they might end up ratting on.

Unless…

"Is Cumberland hiring?"

Helen cleared her throat. "Um, yeah. We're expanding, and we haven't filled Christina's job yet. She was in marketing. Why?"

Winter chewed her lip. "I'm starting to think the only way I'm going to be able to figure what's going on at Cumberland is to actually be there."

"What do you mean?"

"If you were talking to someone who wanted to get a job at Cumberland, what advice would you give them?"

"Wear a short skirt and a push-up bra?"

"I thought you might say something like that." Winter groaned internally. "Listen, Helen. If there's any connection between Aliyah's disappearance, Christina's suicide, and

Nathan Lynch, I will find it. And if there is a connection, the worst thing you could do would be to call off the investigation right now. If Nathan's escalating to kidnapping or worse, then we need to stop him before he hurts anybody else."

"You're right…" She didn't sound convinced. "So you want to go undercover here?"

Want was a strong word. The very idea of putting on a push-up bra so some misogynistic prick could ogle her had Winter's skin crawling. "I think it'd be the best thing for the investigation."

"Okay." It sounded like Helen blew her nose. "Send me your application and make sure you have a headshot on there. They can't legally ask for your picture, but the pretty women who include one get interviews. I'll get it over to Tucker, our HR guy. Tell him you're a friend from my college days at A&M, which he'll only half hear. Doesn't matter where you went, since you're gorgeous. I'm sure he'll want to interview you right away. These guys see a pair of great tits and can't even spell background check."

Is that place a damn cathouse?

"You'll want to study up on some basic climbing terminology, though. Tucker genuinely does like to hire climber girls. I think he has a rope kink."

Winter wasn't sure what to say to that. "Okay. I'll get it over to you soon."

The moment Winter hung up, Ariel rushed inside the office. "You're seriously going undercover?" The unbridled energy she oozed was a little off-putting. Like a puppy tripping all over its human's ankles.

"I can't think of another way to get to the bottom of this thing. At least, not quickly." Winter crossed her arms. "If what Helen suspects turns out to be true, I don't want to leave this guy roaming free for much longer. Or this Tucker guy. The place sounds overrun with dirtbags."

"In that case, we better get started." She set her iPad down on Winter's desk and pressed play on a YouTube video.

Rock Climbing. A Complete Beginner's Guide. Part One.

8

Later that night, Winter sat on the sofa in her living room with two short lengths of rope. She'd always been a hands-on learner. Simply learning a bit of terminology or looking at some pictures did not feel like enough.

She was working on mastering the double fisherman's knot when Kline came over and sat in the chair across from her. Even though she'd invited him to stay, every time he walked into a room, it felt like a stranger was living in her house.

His intense blue eyes—a reflection of her own—made the whole situation feel uncanny. Of course, she knew Kline a bit by this point. He was a contractor from Texas who loved football and despised the internet. He'd weaseled his way into Winter's life long before he came clean about why he was really there.

She knew it was true, but the whole thing still felt like a lie. After all, Kline Hurst wasn't even his real name.

But she'd decided to give him a chance to tell his story in his own time.

Still, she reserved the right to run background checks on Kline Hurst and John Drewitt the second she smelled dishonesty.

"Evenin'." Kline picked at the edges of the bandage around his wounded hand. "Working on some knots?"

"Your sister called me yesterday."

She waited, watching his reaction. It was clear he was trying to keep himself calm. Still, his fingers tightened a bit on the leather arm rest.

"Opal called you?"

"She said her name was Opal. Then again, she said your name was Kline, so I'm not sure if I can trust her."

"I'm not sure what you mean."

Winter set the knotted rope in her lap. "Surely, your sister called you John your whole life. Why would she go along with calling you a different name?"

Kline visibly twitched.

Good.

A little pressure never hurt anybody. If anything, it might keep him honest. She could tell that was a problem for him.

"Opal...well..."

"Why don't you just tell me the truth, hmm?"

"Opal was very helpful with that whole situation."

"Helpful how?"

"I was living in her garage back then. After I took on...a new identity." He inhaled deeply, then exhaled very slowly. Bit by bit, his face grew calm and open.

"Why did you need a new identity?" Like so many times with her so-called father, she wasn't sure what to make of him, but she needed to know how Kline Hurst came to be.

He let out a sigh, and it sounded to Winter like there was heaviness he tried to release with that breath. "I was a drunk, a liar, a cheat. So far down the rabbit hole, I couldn't see daylight. I was out one night on my way to buy more alcohol and…"

Winter waited, not offering any direction. She wanted him to tell whatever story he was going to tell.

"And I saw a pile of clothes, this big lump on the roadway in front of me. I thought I was imaginin' it, but I swerved and ended up in the ditch. Banged up the old car in the process." Kline shook his head. "So I get out, and I walk on over, and it's a man. A dead man. Had to have been a hit and run."

She waited again, but he didn't continue. Watching his face, she knew he was remembering the scene. His jaw clenched and unclenched like he was in pain. She pressed him. "And you just swapped IDs with him? How come the authorities never tracked you down?"

"He was homeless, Winter. I mean, he *lived* on the streets. You could just tell. I didn't just swap lives…" His eyes grew wet, and he paused. "I dragged him off the road so he wouldn't get hit again. I had to make a couple trips. He had bags of dirty clothes, blankets, and there was identification. It fell out of one of his bags." Kline slumped in his seat. "My license had already been suspended, and I saw his, and I just…pocketed it. I didn't even know why at the time."

He seemed to go away after that, like he was dreaming with his eyes open.

"Weren't you worried someone would question you using his name? Recognize it?"

"Sure, I was. I still struggle with it. But as I was looking down at this dead man, something in my head snapped, and I thought, this was my chance. We both had the same build, were close to the same age. It was a clean slate. And right there, John Drewitt died on the side of the road, and Kline Hurst survived."

"You don't drink."

"I quit in that moment too. No one would care about the

death of the screwup John Drewitt, a man who'd wasted his life. But Kline Hurst can fix things. He can build new things, a new life…new relationships. Mend fences." He shrugged, and Winter knew that was the most articulate he could be in the moment.

Her heart broke a little at Kline's confession. "I would've—"

The door off the kitchen banged open like it only ever did when Noah was thundering through it. He was back from a jog.

Winter gave Kline a small nod, stood, and headed through the house. When Noah caught sight of her, he smiled.

He looked only slightly disheveled—sweaty and a bit pink at his cheeks. His brown hair, which had gotten a bit long, was slicked back by sweat, and burgeoning stubble poked out from his chin.

Stepping closer, her husband set his hand on her hip before leaning in and kissing her cheek. "I wondered when you might come home. How's the new cases going?"

"Meh." Winter wanted to confide in him about Kline. About Opal and her DNA running wild on the internet. And about all the misgivings she was feeling about her work plan. She'd sent in her false résumé, and the interview with the HR manager at Cumberland had already been arranged for tomorrow morning.

At the same time, she hesitated. Though he showed nothing but respect for her skills as an agent and an investigator, her husband tended to be very protective. If he knew she was getting all sexed up to go for an interview at a company headed by an alleged rapist, he might be less than thrilled.

"On another note, I got a call yesterday from someone claiming to be my aunt."

"Really?" Noah sat down on the bench by the door and bent to unlace his running shoes. "Kline's sister?"

"So she says. Apparently, she matched to the DNA I'd submitted to the online system."

"You wouldn't submit your DNA to something like that."

"Tell me about it, but somebody did. They go by PJ and are claiming to be a cousin of mine…"

Noah looked up, intensity in his forest-green eyes. "You think it's 'our friend?'"

Our friend was their new moniker for Winter's stalker. In addition to sending creepy anonymous text messages to Winter's phone, the stalker had set up a camera at her grandparents' house and installed spyware on Arial's work computer. They'd switched her to using the iPad while her PC got attention at a repair shop.

Of course, all this was assuming one person was behind it all. It was possible they had more than one friend. They'd even entertained the idea that Kline was responsible, as his entrance into Winter's life hadn't felt random. But then he'd let that particular cat out of the bag on his own.

A chill raced down Winter's spine—that implacable and terrifying feeling of being watched. Even though Noah was covered in sweat and smelling far less appealing than his normal *sweet with a side of musky* aroma, she sat beside him and leaned into his shoulder. "Who else?"

He stroked a hand down her smooth black hair. "What did Kline have to say about the whole thing?"

She shrugged. "What does he say about anything? Sometimes, I'm not sure I care."

"Winter?"

"He's in the living room," she whispered.

"Got it." Noah kissed her forehead.

They'd pick up the Kline conversation later in bed, where she'd update him.

"So how about your case? Any new developments?"

"Well," Winter bit her lip, "you're not allowed to get mad. And you have to understand that this is really the only way."

His face fell, dread clouding his eyes like a converging hurricane. "Oh, I really do not like the sound of that."

9

Cumberland was a casual office. It was better for the company to project an image of athleticism and rocking-climbing know-how than simple professionalism. So although the employees spent nearly all their time sitting behind desks, the standard uniform, for male employees at least, seemed to be jeans or khakis and a button-down shirt.

Last night, when she was feeling apprehensive, Winter had texted Helen to ask what qualities in a woman would appeal to Cumberland's hiring manager. Not surprisingly, her tips had nothing to do with knowledge, skills, or expertise.

Short shorts, a tight shirt. Wear your hair down. Make sure you do your makeup. Tucker especially loves red lips.

The specificity had left Winter feeling a bit sick through most of the night. She didn't always respond well to unwanted attention from men. Having spent a career surrounded by testosterone-flooded tough guys, she had no problem standing up for herself. It was just that her instinctive response to a lurid stare or suggestive comment was to knock a guy's teeth down his throat.

That would be less than conducive to her goals.

When she got dressed that morning in high-waisted short shorts and a white button-down that showed the barest hint of a forest-green bra beneath—it was St. Paddy's Day, after all—Winter looked at herself in the mirror, then had to go hide in her walk-in closet, away from any and all reflective surfaces.

"I can't live with or without you, Sissy." Her brother's voice echoed in her head, his sharp eyes wandering up and down her body. His hands on her breasts. She was tied up and couldn't get away from him. *"Been a while since I've been with a woman. I've been trying to figure out if I should break my fast with your or pretty little Nicole. Right now, I'd say I'm leaning in one delicious direction."*

Winter shuddered. She slammed those doors in her mind and secured them with iron locks, fighting to keep herself in the moment. She threw on her hiking boots and rushed out to her Honda Pilot, inserting the key in the ignition before the door was even closed.

Thank goodness Noah wasn't there when she left for the day. He'd had words about her plan last night, and he would've had a lot more to say this morning, especially after seeing her outfit. Though he would never dare to forbid her from doing something, she'd seen the vague sadness in his eyes. It was the fear he carried with him everywhere since the day Justin kidnapped her.

She kept the speedometer high and humming all the way to Cumberland, avoiding her own overly made-up eyes in the rearview mirror.

When Winter arrived, she sat in the SUV, frozen. The office was a large and very fancy prefab build, set on gorgeously maintained grounds covered with flowers and trees. Little paths of sandstone wove among bushes, and a tall rappelling tower loomed out back.

After a few steadying breaths, she stepped out onto the asphalt. She tugged down the hem of her short shorts and made her way along the winding path toward the glass double doors.

Stepping inside, she had to pause at the grandeur of the place. The vaulted ceiling was a good three stories high, every wall made of rainbowed sandstone. With the air conditioner cranked, a faint buzz vibrated the building. A huge fountain trickled over an open wall, but everywhere else had climbing holds, even on the ceiling. Ropes hung here and there, ready to assist.

At the center of the room stood a sales display with products and pretty posters. Not unlike the dress code, Cumberland's offices promised adventure with a touch of luxury. A climb to a summit to eat Brie and drink red wine.

Winter made her way across the echoey room and introduced herself to a very young and pretty receptionist seated behind a small desk. A nameplate read *Dawn Goodan*. The young woman checked her name in the appointment book, then asked her to have a seat.

Winter waited in a little leather chair, her eyes wandering about the room. She reminded herself why she was there and why she had to do this. One woman was dead. Another was missing. Instead of worrying about her own situation, she needed to remember the women in this office who weren't highly trained, ex-FBI, undercover private investigators. Women like Helen Marchand, Christina Norris, Aliyah Andry, and this young receptionist Dawn Goodan.

They were the reason she was here.

"Be friendly." Helen had said that. *"Smile. Laugh at his stupid jokes."*

"Samantha?" a man's voice called out.

Winter almost forgot that was her name.

"Yes?" She stood and turned toward the man with what she hoped looked like an eager smile on her lips.

"I'm Tucker Hicks, the hiring manager." He offered his hand. "Nice to meet you."

"Nice to meet you too. It's great to be here."

He was about six feet tall, average build. He had a scruffy mountain nerd thing going on. Black-rimmed glasses, a trim beard, meticulously disheveled hair. He wore jeans and a lime-green sports coat over an old flannel shirt.

"Come on back."

Winter followed him down a wide hallway and past posters of previous Cumberland ads. A few old mountain bikes were hung high up as art.

They came into a conference room with a long table of natural wood down the center. Tucker gestured for her to have a seat, then clicked a button on a remote. A projector cast a blue screen onto a blank white wall.

"Just a short training video, and then we'll begin the interview."

"Okay. Great." Winter smiled, then fixed her eyes on the video like she gave a shit.

"Welcome to Cumberland, one of the leading providers of outdoor and mountain climbing equipment. In this video, you'll learn about our company and everything you need to know to serve our customers and our mission. Now gear up! Let's go!"

The video showed a montage of stunning outdoor and mountain-climbing footage. Winter kept her eyes trained to the video, but in her periphery, she saw Tucker standing off to one side, phone in his hand, fiddling away. But he kept glancing up from it. And not to watch the video.

"Cumberland is dedicated to providing outdoor enthusiasts with the highest quality gear and equipment for their adventures. Our mission is to inspire and enable people to explore the great outdoors with confidence and safety. As an employee, you play a crucial role

in delivering exceptional service and ensuring our customers have memorable experiences."

The video went on like that. Winter listened intently, focused on memorizing every word. She was going to be a good employee. Or at least, pretend to be one.

"To excel in your role, it's essential to have a thorough understanding of our products. Take the time to familiarize yourself with the features, benefits, and usage of each item we offer." The video showed a man with chalked hands tying an elaborate knot into a line of nylon rope. *"This knowledge will enable you to answer customer questions confidently and assist them in finding the perfect gear for their adventures."*

Tucker stepped closer and slid into a chair at her side. She could feel him openly staring at her. She wanted her to cross her legs, button the top of her shirt, and punch him right in his leering eyes.

But she did none of those things. Instead, she glanced at him, flashed a shy smile, then looked back at the screen.

The rest of the video passed with a string of cheesy maxims. Winter could barely hear the words. She'd expected a bit of ogling, some thinly veiled misogyny. But the way this man was staring at her made her feel like he was already trying to take off her clothes.

"So does this still seem like something you'd be interested in?" Tucker asked with a half-cocked smile.

"Yes, absolutely."

"What's your experience with climbing?"

"I don't have much on an actual mountain. I've done a lot of climbing at the gym, and a little back in college with Helen, but that's about it."

"That's okay. I'd be happy to take you out sometime, just so you have some experience."

It would be a cold day in hell before Winter went with

this guy into the mountains or anywhere not mandated by her investigation. "That'd be great."

"All right. Well, I like your résumé. And I think you have good energy. You'll fit in here just fine."

That was it. The whole interview. No background check necessary.

He stood and shook her hand, holding her grasp several seconds longer than necessary. "I'll have to have a chat with our CEO to confirm, but as far as I'm concerned, you're hired."

"Really?" Winter got to her feet, fighting the urge to yank her hand out of Tucker's. "Thank you so much."

"You're going to be working in sales under Melissa Hinds. She's our marketing executive. I'll take you down to meet her."

"I'm so excited." She pasted a wide smile on her face.

Tucker's eyes dipped down to her cleavage and didn't come back up. "Excellent. We love excited around here."

Winter followed Tucker farther down the hall to the open door of a large office. He stepped up to a woman seated at a desk and set his hand lightly on her back. "Melissa, I'd like you to meet Samantha. She's going to be your new underling."

Melissa smiled. She was very beautiful, with long, straight blond hair and golden skin. In her mid-thirties, Winter guessed, as her skin was a little leathery under all her makeup—the way it got when someone spent a lot of time in the sun. Clearly, Melissa walked the walk when it came to mountaineering. Or climbed the climb.

After initial introductions, Tucker stepped up behind Winter. "I'll leave you in Melissa's capable hands." Before he left, he set his hand on the small of Winter's back and let it linger. Her spine tried to tighten, her fist along with it. She forced herself loose.

When he was gone, Melissa turned back to her computer. "I am so sorry, Samantha. I didn't know I was getting a new person today. I'm not quite ready to train you. Give me just a few minutes to wrap up what I'm doing here."

"No problem. I wasn't expecting to get a job today." She sat in a chair opposite Melissa's desk, holding her bag on her lap. "Tucker doesn't like to waste any time, does he?"

"You have no idea." There was a twist in the corner of Melissa's lips that looked a bit like a smile. Still, her words landed on Winter like lead weights.

Winter had the distinct impression Nathan Lynch wasn't the only man at Cumberland who was taking advantage of his position.

"So what's it like working here?"

Melissa kept her eyes glued to her computer screen as she answered. "It's not bad. Nathan takes good care of his people. He expects a lot, but he gives a lot."

"That's the big boss, right?"

"Yeah." Melissa scoffed lightly. "You'd better learn his name."

"What does he expect?"

"Always look your best, for one. But Nathan'll want to tell you himself about everything he'll expect. I think he's in his office right now. Why don't you go say hi while I finish up here?"

"Okay…" Winter didn't like the sound of that. And she didn't like the small tremor in her own voice. She cleared her throat. "Which way?"

"Keep going down the hall all the way to the end. The big corner office."

Nodding, Winter slipped out of Melissa's office and continued down the hall. The footprint of the one-story building was huge—part factory, part McMansion, part hunting lodge. She found the glass doors of the CEO's office easily but stopped herself from knocking.

Do your job. Don't be a baby.

She fluffed the back of her hair and went to his door, rapping timorously on the outside.

"Yes?" a man called from within.

Winter approached the desk.

Nathan Lynch looked just like his picture, and he smelled like expensive cologne.

When he saw Winter, his eyebrows lifted. "Hello. What can I do for you?"

"Hi." Winter forced blush into her cheeks and kept her body language small and submissive, clasping her hands behind her back. "I just had an interview with Tucker and met Melissa, who I'll be working under. She said I should come meet you."

"I see." He clicked off the screen of the phone in his hand and set it face down on the desk. He extended his hand. "Nathan Lynch."

"Samantha Drewitt. You can call me Sam."

"Sam." He smiled. "You ought to know that working at Cumberland can be quite a commitment. I need all my employees to be dedicated and trustworthy. We're still a small company, but expanding, so sometimes getting the job done means staying late."

"I understand. That's not a problem."

"Do you have a family at home?"

Is this still part of the interview? Because that's an illegal question.

"No, I'm not married." Winter shook her head. She tried to think about that time Noah danced for her in nothing but cowboy boots in the hopes of bringing some blush to her cheeks. "I've heard of you before. I used to work at Carmean Sports."

His face brightened at the sound of his former workplace. "Really? Must've been after I was gone. I'm sure I would've remembered you."

She nodded shyly. "There's a lot of stories about you, about your career. While I'm here, I'd love to learn more."

He leaned back in his chair, looking very pleased with himself. "Oh?"

"I think you'd be a great mentor."

"I'm honored." Unlike Tucker, who stared openly with no finesse, Nathan took in her body in quick, plausibly deniable glimpses. Still just enough that she could feel the heat of his eyes nowhere and everywhere all at once. "Tell you what. First you show me you have potential worth mentoring, then we can talk."

"Thank you. I will."

With one last, sweet smile, Winter turned to leave. She was so focused on the predator she was escaping from that she didn't notice the man coming into his office. She bumped into him with a yelp.

Winter's instinct was to break his arm for touching her, accidental as it might've been. But even she had to admit that was a little extreme.

"Excuse me." The man stepped back and cast his eyes down. "Are you okay?"

Winter nodded, appreciating that at least one man in Cumberland wasn't eye-humping her like a model in a skimpy dress at a car show.

"I'm fine. My fault." She cast one last smile at Nathan, then continued through the door.

"What do you need, Bryan?" Nathan asked, sounding bored.

"I'm knocking off early. I want to hit the rocks."

"Whatever. Just get the TPC report to me before you go."

Outside Melissa's office, Winter saw the woman still

deeply engaged in work, so she walked straight past her, out the door, and into the gorgeous, landscaped gardens. The warmth of the sun was just enough to chase the icy feeling from her skin.

She took out her phone and dialed Ariel, who picked up after the first ring.

"How's it going over there?"

"It's…" She wasn't sure how to finish that sentence. "Can you get me a list of climbing places near Austin? I want both gyms and outside areas."

"No problem. I think first you might want to check out El Barranco State Park."

"Oh, yeah? Why?"

"'Cause a Cumberland employee was found dead there at the bottom of a gorge."

10

As soon as she could escape from the Cumberland complex, which was sooner than she'd expected, Winter left for the wilderness preserve outside Austin. A fairly maintained dirt, double-lane road led her alongside the twists of a small river, swollen from the rain. Her maps app was not especially helpful, and she had to rely on the written directions Ariel had provided.

The natural beauty of the space was striking. Sheer cliff faces jutted up from the forest bed. She cracked the window and let the fresh air rush over her as the smell of pine and rainwater tickled her nose. The wind rushed through her hair. She slowed down, savoring the peace of the ride before she arrived at the murder scene.

The body of Parker Roy, once a Cumberland employee, had been discovered at the bottom of a ravine by some crack-of-dawn sportsperson with an especially curious dog. Winter had found out what few details she could when the buzz of Parker Roy's death was starting to make its way around the office. The thirty one year old had been a salesperson for Cumberland for the past four years. He was a bachelor who lived alone and wasn't dating as far as anyone knew.

She pulled into a very small lot at the end of the dirt road, which was covered in pea gravel. Her Pilot had barely made it, nearly skidding out twice and leaving her heart pounding. If she came back out again, she was definitely asking Noah to borrow the truck.

A huge white truck was already parked there, the emblem of the Texas Parks and Wildlife Department printed on the side. Exiting her vehicle, Winter caught sight of yellow crime scene tape sectioning off an area of tree line.

Since she was still dressed in her overly provocative shorts and tight button-down, Winter took Noah's windbreaker that he'd left in her back seat and pulled it on, zipping it up to her neck. She tied back her hair and pulled on a baseball cap. Luckily, proper hiking boots were part of the Cumberland standard uniform, so she was good to go there.

As she stepped toward the crime scene, the door of the truck popped open, and a man in a khaki uniform stepped out. "Ma'am? Excuse me? You can't go down there. This is an active crime scene."

A circular badge bearing a five-pointed star in the center was pinned to his greige shirt, the outer edge showing *Texas Parks and Wildlife State Park Police*, and his bronze name tag read *Deputy L. Mullaney*. The first thing that struck her about him was his height. Six-five, at least. The kind of tall that stretched the face and limbs, leaving no meat for the bones. His protruding Adam's apple twitched with each breath as his hooded brown eyes watched her carefully from under his white straw cowboy hat.

"Hi. My name is Winter Black." She stepped toward him and offered her hand. "I'm a private investigator.

"Nice to meet you." That sounded like a lie.

"I've been hired to look into some potential criminal activity taking place at your victim's place of work. Maybe we could help each other."

He looked as suspicious as a housefly rubbing its hands together. Winter knew that look, so she went into her glove compartment and showed him her credentials.

After scrutinizing every piece of paper she gave him, the deputy looked up with recognition in his eyes. "I've heard of you."

"Oh?" That wasn't always a good thing.

"Winter Black, FBI. You worked The Prodigy case."

She cringed inwardly, as she always did when she heard the horrible moniker the media had bestowed on her murderous little brother. "That's right."

"I studied that case in college."

She nearly balked. "Really? How old are you?"

"I'll be twenty-two in three weeks."

Winter had never felt so old in all her life. He was just a baby, and she was a weary old agent whose cases he studied in his baby school.

Still, the feeling was vastly preferable to the way Tucker Hicks and Nathan Lynch had made her feel just a few hours ago. Like a teenager about to be taken advantage of.

"I think there might be a connection between this and what I've been working on. Can I get a look at the scene?"

"That might be difficult."

That answer surprised Winter. One of the joys of being the veteran was that rookies were supposed to leap at the opportunity to work with someone like her. "I won't disturb anything. And I've been deputized by APD for cases in the past. Detective Davenport would vouch for me."

He might bitch and moan the entire time, but she was confident her exasperated PD contact still saw the value in her expertise, despite the extra paperwork she always made for him and everybody else involved.

"No, no. That's fine. I'll throw you in the supplemental reports, and we're good to go. But I mean, the scene is kind of difficult to get down to. I'll show you."

Deputy Mullaney turned and started toward the line of yellow tape, Winter close behind. Immediately, they left the trail. Prickly understory nipped at her exposed legs, so she had to pick her way through like a nervous stork.

"We haven't found any tire tracks we can confirm," Mullaney called back to her. Head down and shoulders hunched, he fought to keep from braining himself on every passing limb. "We know it had to be a four-wheel drive."

"You can't get up here without it." Her Honda had AWD, and she'd barely been able to crawl over the twisty rocks and gravel.

"Exactly. Also, to say he died of strangulation is a bit of an understatement."

Strangled to death. Noted.

He paused at the edge of a ravine, bushy trees obscuring the bottom. Nylon rope was tied off around a boulder, the coils wrapping around the giant rock over and over again. Mullaney picked up the rope and peered downward. "Have you ever done any rappelling?"

She bit the corner of her lip and looked down. She couldn't say for certain how deep the crevice was. One hundred feet, maybe more. "Not since the academy."

"We'll have to climb back up, of course. I got a knot ladder hung. Or you can go the really long away around. There's a hiking trail that leads down."

The really long way sounded like a huge waste of time. Besides, Winter's hands twitched at the thrill of a new challenge.

She knew she was strong enough. Not only did she hit the

gym almost obsessively—due to her persistent need to be strong enough to tie the average man into knots—she often DIY'd her own warrior courses with rocks and logs and playground equipment when she went jogging. Finding jumps and holds and crawls and whatever she could to keep herself ready for anything.

She'd been called paranoid.

"That's fine. I'm game."

Mullaney went to the boulder and opened a plastic chest that looked a bit like a cooler. He rummaged around, retrieved a rappelling harness and helmet, and passed them over.

Last night, when working on learning her ropes, she'd gotten reacquainted with rappelling. Waist strap snug to squeeze and catch you. Leg loops positioned for a comfortable sit. There were built-in hard points for the climbing rope and a belay loop.

"It's not too far, but watch out for the branches. If one catches you, it'll rip you apart." Mullaney tied his own harness into the rope with a figure-eight knot. "I got an auto-belay mounted, but don't rely on that. It's more of a fail-safe. This is all you. And me, I guess." He giggled nervously, then stifled it. "I'll go down first."

Winter studied him as he stepped up to the ledge, his back to the descent.

Using his grip on the rope and its hold in the harness, Deputy Mullaney slowly lowered himself into an *L* at the lip of the rappel point, like sitting with his back against a wall and legs out in front of him. Except, of course, there was no wall, and his feet were the only things touching ground. Then he used the rope and a controlled release of slack to descend.

"Easy peasy," Winter said out loud, partly to convince herself that it was true. "Monkey see, monkey do."

She clipped on and backed up to the ledge, her hand tight on the rope. The rush she'd felt earlier intensified as she sat back over the edge. As she glanced down, the little bubbles of stress that had been clinging to the edges of her brain began to burst. With a deep breath, she positioned one foot, then the other.

Her hand was in defiance of the rest of her, refusing to loosen on the rope that held her fixed. Winter took a deep breath. *I'm not afraid of heights. I'm not afraid of anything. I am a damn warrior.*

At last, her fingers were convinced. She loosened her grip and pushed off with her feet into a controlled free fall, then caught the wall again on her boots. Her stomach leaped into her throat in the most pleasant way. For a few moments as she made her way down the cliff, her brain emptied itself of every thought, except for those she needed to keep going, keep moving.

Maybe all those rock climbing nerds at Cumberland were onto something.

The bottom of the ravine was littered with sharp rocks and dead wood. When the soles of her boots touched down, she wobbled, feeling pleasantly drunk for exactly five seconds. Normally, Winter did not experience an adrenaline rush unless it was accompanied by the threat of impending trauma. She rarely got to enjoy that pure, unadulterated high without her life being in danger. She laughed and looked up at how far she'd come.

"I'm not afraid of heights," she said out loud, only this time she meant it. "I'm a damn warrior!"

"What?" Mullaney looked over his shoulder from where he stood among the brush, several yards away.

"Nothing." She struggled with the carbine to unhook herself, then jogged to catch up with the deputy. She felt lighter than air, like if she jumped hard enough, she might float off into the branches.

Mullaney checked his watch. "The body was found here around, well, almost a dozen hours ago." He stepped under yellow tape between a few sharp boulders, some of which were clearly stained with blood. "It sustained a lot of damage when it was dropped, but he was dead long before then. The M.E. is still working out what was pre- and postmortem."

Winter nodded and circled the area, gently setting one boot in front of the other to stay balanced. She noticed little nicks of red and orange tape pasted to trees and boulders and going up the wall she's just rappelled down. "What do these mean?"

"The parks department wasn't able to confirm this as an official climbing route. A climber left them for himself so he could find the place again."

She stepped closer to a trunk and hovered her fingers over the photo-degraded tape. The placement was very deliberate, each strip exactly the same size and running perfectly parallel to the ground. "Maybe there's something to this place."

"What do you mean?"

"I mean, maybe this isn't just a random ravine. Maybe this place means something to the killer." She turned back to Mullaney with a shrug. "You said he was strangled?"

"That's putting it mildly." Mullaney grimaced. "He was bound in so many knots, I'm sure he couldn't even move."

"Rock climbing knots?"

"They were definitely tied by somebody who knew what they were doing."

"Do you have a lot of experience with climbing?"

"Sure." Mullaney puffed out his chest. "I learned in the scouts."

Of course he did. *When was that? Last week?*

"Can I get a look at the crime scene photos?"

"Yeah, I can probably manage that." He stuffed his hand into one of his pockets and pulled out his phone. "Here. I took a few to study the system this killer used to tie his victim. You never know what you might learn from it."

Winter smiled. This kid took his job seriously. She liked that in a person.

What she did not like were those photos. Parker Roy had been bound by a pro in a contraption that looked like something Houdini would've tried to escape from. It was bright-green rope. Gruesomely festive. She'd seen a bin of similar rope beside Nathan Lynch's desk, but that didn't necessarily mean anything.

Mullaney was pointing out the types of knots—but Winter wasn't listening anymore. Beyond the crest of the yellow police tape, a faint red glow had arrested her attention.

It had taken some time, but Winter had learned never to ignore the glow. The glow came to her at sporadic moments, guiding her toward details that always ended up being significant in one way or another.

Her ability to see the glow was a parting gift from the monster who'd taken her family and transformed her baby brother into the twisted killer he was today. The injuries Winter suffered at his hands had forced her to undergo brain surgery as a child, and when she woke up, she'd had a new sense. A special way of looking at the world.

Or at least, that was what she'd always believed until she met Kline. He had the gift, too, according to him, but with no scars on his skull. Now she was left wondering if the whole injury-and-surgery ordeal was just a coincidence.

The glow sometimes came alone—a beacon. Other times, she would be incapacitated by the sight of it. Pain would spread all through her brain, her nose would bleed, and visions would overtake her.

Winter excused herself and stepped toward the glowing rock.

"Goes without saying, don't disturb the scene." Mullaney called after her. It wasn't an order, more a gentle reminder. Like telling a three year old not to eat a bug.

Ducking under the tape, she moved among the brambles, ignoring the sharp burrs that delivered little white scratches to her thighs. There, among a pile of boulders, was the glowing object. A thick tangle of nylon rope.

"Deputy Mullaney!" Winter knelt beside the ropes. Her fingers tingled with the desire to take them into her hands and turn them over, but she'd never disturb the scene. She kept her elbows on her knees to avoid touching even a single rock. The way it looped back on itself, the rope resembled a heavy fishing net.

As she studied it from different angles, she thought she recognized some of the knots. Clove hitches, double fisherman, and arbor loops. Figure eights. And not just from her quick tutorials. Mullaney had just mentioned them.

He peeked through the brush, then his booted feet approached heavily. It was only as he stepped up to her side that Winter recognized dark-red stains on the rope mantle near the site of a very clumsy cut.

"Geez." He went into the pocket of his cargo shorts and took out a large plastic bag and a glove, which he held out to Winter. "That's the same rope Parker Roy was tied with."

Winter nodded. "It looks brand new." She put on the neoprene glove, bagged the rope, and took a step back, squinting as she turned her eyes over the ravine. "Maybe there was another victim."

"Looks like it."

Winter noticed a thicker patch of bright-green fibers on

the edge of a very sharp rock jutting up from some roots in the packed earth. She stepped closer and knelt beside it. Flecks of blood stained the dirt like droplets of motor oil. She pointed at the fibers clinging to the sharp rock. "They cut their binds and crawled off into the wilderness."

He looked around. "Yeah. That's possible."

Turning her gaze to the sky, she took a shaky breath. "The killer thought this person was dead. He threw them down here along with Parker Roy."

"You think somebody survived that?" Mullaney sounded incredulous.

"A missing persons report was filed Tuesday morning on an Aliyah Andry. Her vehicle was found open with her keys on the ground at Marburg Accounting."

"I'm not following."

"She left Cumberland a month ago and has a possible connection to the criminal activity I've been hired to look into at the company."

"Now I'm following. Aliyah Andry, you say?"

"Yes, and look." Winter pointed to some branches jutting out of the cliff about twenty or so feet up. One of them appeared to be broken and facing downward. "If they hit a few branches on the way down and landed on their side, they'd be in bad shape, but...yes. They survived." A painful twinge of empathy ripped through her bones.

"Holy mama..." Mullaney's jaw hung slack, then he snatched the radio from his belt and called in what they'd discovered.

The Park Ranger Law Enforcement Academy did not mess around when they trained their recruits, and within the hour, a dozen rangers had rappelled down that hundred-foot cliff wall and were hunting for the second victim.

The M.E. arrived, too, to collect blood samples from the rocks.

Before everyone showed up, Winter and Mullaney had found what appeared to be several narrow tracks in the earth. The prints looked like they were from a shoe, a small one, and the furrows on the right were longer, an indication that the victim was dragging their leg.

Ground Search and Rescue began rallying from up top. And she heard the faint whir of a helicopter coming in. If this was Aliyah Andry, she'd been presumed missing since Monday night, almost forty-eight hours ago, and daylight was not on their side.

Winter climbed up the rope ladder, having done all she could down below. Mullaney stayed with his fellow officers to partake in the search.

At the top, the search and rescue team consisted of about twenty-five people, split into five teams, each group poring over a map they'd divided into quadrants, gaining fast acquaintance with their assigned locations. Two teams lined up to rappel down the cliff to the last known position of the second victim to branch out from there until nightfall. The others dispersed to widen the search.

Winter watched as the final team members clipped on and held tight to the rope as they backed to the cliff's ledge and went down.

She feared in her heart the missing person was Aliyah. But no matter who it was, time was running out to find them alive.

11

The gray blue of twilight was all around her when Winter returned to her office and settled behind her desk. As often happened, she'd underestimated the case when she took it on. Sexual harassment and a young woman's suicide were bad enough, but with one of Cumberland's employees found dead in the woods, and another dead or possibly injured and alone in the vast wilderness, she was going to have to give the investigation her full attention.

"Ariel!" she called, not looking up as she clicked open her browser.

Her stalwart assistant was in the doorway in a flash and still pretty bouncy for the late hour. "Yes?"

"Going undercover at Cumberland's going to take up my days for the foreseeable future, so I'm going to need you to run the office and keep in contact with my other clients."

"Of course." Her permanent smile broadened. "That's my job, right?"

"I might end up having to cancel some upcoming appointments, so I'll need you to go through the books and make some calls."

"You got it."

Winter typed the name *Aliyah Andry* into her favorite deep-search program. "If there's anything needing my personal attention, I'll only be able to get to it after five every day. Hopefully, around five or six. Thanks for staying, by the way."

"Absolutely. And you don't need to worry about anything. I've got you covered."

At times, Winter got annoyed by Ariel's unflappable confidence and cheery desire to take on as much responsibility as possible. But right now, her enthusiasm was a godsend.

"And I also need you to keep digging into Nathan Lynch."

"I already have." She stepped closer to the desk, her brown curls bouncing. Then she set her iPad down in front of Winter. "Well, you know that window of time when Lynch wasn't working?"

Winter cocked her head.

"Apparently, his mother died, and he left for the Himalayas to meditate. For like a year."

"What?" Winter wasn't often surprised by anybody's background, but this was odd. "Like the Beatles?"

"Yeah, and a lot of good that did. Check this out." Ariel pulled up a document—a court briefing. *Plaintiff Parker Roy. Defendant Cumberland Mountain Equipment Company, LLC, and Nathan Lynch, CEO.*

"What's this?" Winter set one finger against the screen, dirt still packed under the nail from her impromptu mountaineering excursion.

"Roy accused Lynch of sexual harassment and filed suit against him and the company."

Legalese always gave Winter a headache, the way the words went on and on without saying anything, couching all pertinent information in two-ton piles of bullshit. She gestured for Ariel to get on with it.

"Parker Roy claimed hostile work environment." Ariel scrolled through the document on her iPad. "He cited repeated instances of Nathan Lynch making inappropriate comments toward him, degrading him in front of the other employees and customers."

"Well, now, that's not very Zen of him." Winter leaned back in her chair, raising a fresh coffee to her lips. "Give me an example."

"Oh, you know. Making fun of the size of his…giggle stick."

Winter choked on her coffee. "His what?"

"His tickle pickle."

"That is so vulgar." Winter wiped a hand over her face. "Can you just say penis, please?"

Ariel's freckles darkened with the whisper of a blush. "Lynch also implied Roy couldn't get it up and didn't know how to please a woman. Said he was gay, and he wasn't. You know. Classic macho locker-room bull."

"You got a pic of Parker Roy?" Mullaney hadn't taken any of his face, and Winter wanted to see the victim with some blood running through his veins.

"Uh, yeah. Sure." A little wrinkle formed on Ariel's nose, exposing her confusion, but she picked up her iPad and flicked around a bit before setting it back down on Winter's desk.

Just as Winter had suspected, Parker Roy had been a very good-looking man. Tall, blond, tan. Every inch of his body was hard and sharp from his slightly asymmetrical Ryan Gosling chin to his huge hands. In the picture, he was standing sideways on a rock, held in place by a climbing rope at his waist, the sun glistening on his skin.

Nathan Lynch had a cool confidence about him. That was

the first thing Winter had noticed in his presence. A rich boy attitude of *I own the world and everybody in it*. Men like that made a point of belittling anybody they saw as potential competition. And Roy looked like he could've given Lynch a run for his money.

Winter turned her gaze back to Ariel. "So what happened?"

"The case was dropped."

"Cumberland paid him off?"

"Technically, no. The suit against Cumberland was dropped. But a private suit Roy filed against Lynch was settled out of court for an undisclosed amount, and the records were sealed."

"So Nathan Lynch paid him off…" She drummed her fingers on Parker Roy's picture. It was a rare killer who went after a fit young man in his prime. Like any predator, human killers tended to assess the risk of going after such prey as far too great. Most tended more toward the very young or very old. The vulnerable and physically weak.

It would take a special kind of killer to tackle someone like Parker Roy. Most likely, they had a well-constructed plan for how to subdue him and were quite physically strong themselves. Like Nathan Lynch or Tucker Hicks or any of the men who worked at Cumberland.

More than that, everything about this murder, from the choice of victim to the manner of death, suggested premeditation. Whoever killed him had an axe to grind.

Maybe Roy had violated the terms of his settlement with the Cumberland CEO and started blabbing. Where money failed, was it possible Nathan Lynch would've turned to brute force to protect his fragile corporate reputation?

It wasn't much of a stretch.

In Winter's periphery, a shadow on the street approached the glass door of the office. She tensed, her brain envisioning the Smith & Wesson pistol stashed in the top right drawer of her desk. It wasn't that she really thought she needed it—simply a nervous habit of a mind that refused to be a victim ever again.

She recognized the disheveled hair and thick shoulders of her husband as he stepped inside. Her tension vanished, and she rose to her feet. "Keep digging. See if you can find any other suits filed against Lynch or the other companies he's worked for."

"You got it, Boss." Ariel nodded and jogged the few steps back to her desk, brushing by Noah with a polite nod as he stepped into Winter's office.

His sexy eyes scanned her short shorts and his own oversize jacket covering her torso. "Well, hello, there."

Winter almost blushed. Only Noah could ever make her blush. "Seriously? Did you miss all the tiny scratch marks on these legs and my sweaty faded makeup from this morning?"

He stepped closer, snaked a hand around her waist and kissed her lips. Part of her wanted to melt against him, like always. His scent was better than fresh rain on a warm day. It set both her feet firmly on the ground, tied her to the present, away from worries about the future and fears from the past.

All she ever really needed to feel at home was Noah's hands on her waist. The house, the picket fence…all that was just a bonus.

"You look perfect to me."

After pressing into him for a beat, Winter pulled back. "What are you doing here?"

"I dropped by to see if there's anything I could do to help with your investigation. So I can get you home and in our bed before midnight."

Winter smiled but then eyed him suspiciously.

He rolled his eyes. "Don't give me the face."

"You're getting yourself in trouble again, aren't you?"

"That's rich, coming from you."

"Hey, I'm not the one getting put on paid leave."

"Ain't like you're gonna put yourself on leave."

"I would if I felt I deserved it."

"Lies!"

"All right." Taking his hand, Winter led him to a little mid-century loveseat against one glass wall, and they sat down together. "I'm always happy to have you. But I don't want you overstepping your bounds."

"No flirting with the boss, then?" He wiggled his eyebrows.

"You can't keep using FBI resources on my cases. You do all these naughty things I don't ask you to do, and then I get the blame for it."

"Nobody's blaming you."

"Oh, yes, they are. I am."

"I promise. I'm not an agent right now. Just look at me as an enthusiastic unpaid intern."

"My favorite kind." She fought the smile tugging at the corners of her lips, but it was useless. How did he always manage to make her smile even when the whole world seemed dark and depraved? It was his own special kind of magic.

"There's a woman missing, Aliyah Andry, a former Cumberland employee." Winter flexed her fingers. "And today, when I went by the scene where Parker Roy's body was found, the glow led me to a second set of ropes."

"Should I just nod along and pretend I know what that means?"

"The killer ties up his victim with climbing rope. Dozens of knots. That's how Parker Roy was found, wrapped up in this complicated rig." She leaned forward. "And I found a second set of ropes right near the scene. I mean, not twenty feet away."

Noah's face pulled in, eyes and lips narrowing. His thinking face. She knew it well. "So you figure Aliyah Andry got in the same way as Parker Roy but managed to escape."

Winter nodded. "The killer thought she was dead and disposed of her just like Roy. Off a cliff. Maybe trees slowed her fall on the way down. Then she found a sharp rock and sawed through her ropes. Rangers and Search and Rescue are on it. We haven't verified the victim as Aliyah Andry, but I think it's her, and she's out there somewhere. Injured and terrified."

"She doesn't know how lucky she is."

"What do you mean?"

"She's got you." Noah squeezed her hand. "And that means she and this killer are going to be found."

The vote of confidence boosted Winter up and knocked her down all at once. "God, I hope so. I did a quick image search, which I haven't studied yet, but every photo that popped up showed her either outside or on a rock face. She's young and fit as hell."

"Good. Do you think the killer's somebody at Cumberland?"

She chewed on the inside of her cheek, knowing where this was going. "I think the killer's a physically strong and experienced climber. And he's killing people who've worked for Cumberland."

Noah stroked her palm. "I don't like you being on your own in that place. What if the killer finds out who you are and what you're doing there?"

"I won't let that happen." *Well, not unless it would be useful to the investigation.*

"Maybe I could get a job there too. Keep an eye on you."

She had to laugh at that. "Nathan Lynch would *never* hire you."

"Why not? I can climb rocks. I'm sure I can."

"I don't doubt it, but you are way too sexy. You'd intimidate the hell out of him. And I'm getting the impression he's not a guy who can handle competition."

Noah smirked. "I could snap him like a twig, couldn't I?"

"Of course you could, baby." She patted his cheek.

"Is this your uniform?" His eyes scanned down her body, over her legs, then back to her eyes. "What you got on under that jacket?"

This time she really did blush. "Nothing."

"Nothing?" His eyes drank her in, growing greener with every breath. "Can I see?"

Winter glanced at Ariel through the glass wall of her office, then at the privacy blinds pulled up to the ceiling, then back at her husband who was clearly in a mood.

She was in a mood, too—brought on by rappelling down those rocks, then pulling herself back up on knotted rope with the strength of her own arms, leaving her muscles like jelly.

For weeks now, since learning somebody was following her, Winter had been feeling weak and exposed—at the mercy of forces she couldn't control. But today on that ravine wall, she'd felt powerful. And power, as it turned out, was exactly what she needed.

"Go on, then." Winter set her hand on her husband's thigh and flicked her gaze back to the blinds. "You're the only person I want to see me in this outfit."

Noah showed a boyish grin and went to his task with a happy spring in his step, as Winter laughed and leaned back on the loveseat.

12

Aliyah's very loose plan since night one had been to get to the stream in the ravine and follow it until it opened to a river, then walk along that, veering southeast until she hit civilization. Though conventional wisdom would have her stay in one spot until she was rescued, she preferred not to wait around for her attacker to track her down and finish the job.

He was well-built, strong, and knowledgeable about knots. The contraption he'd bound her in was composed of a series of expert-level knots and loops that all worked together like a complex pulley system.

It was some seriously sick medieval shit—what he'd done to her.

And after he'd bound her—as if that hadn't been terrifying enough—he'd driven her into the wilderness and tossed her off a hundred-foot cliff.

On the way down, she'd hit a string of bushy branches and had even gotten caught on two of them. She was certain the second one, an old-as-dirt Ashe Juniper that had cradled her from twenty feet up, had saved her life.

Once it gave way, the branches bending and breaking under her weight, she slid down the rest of the cliff below it, at about a seventy-degree angle, where she rolled over cacti, wildflowers, and saplings until she slammed into an old cypress tree. She was sure her hip was fractured from that collision. But it was better than her head.

The first few hours after that were divided pretty evenly between crying and praying—the opposite of numbing herself with red wine 'til she passed out. In fact, she'd never felt more awake than she had on that first night alone in the vast wilderness.

Freezing, bleeding, itching from the ropes, suffering all-over, car-crash-level pain, all while being terrified her assailant or a mountain lion would find her and finish her off, she spent that first night in helpless agony.

Movement tightened the ropes, cranking the nightmare to the next level, increasing her pain, and reducing her capacity to breathe. So she finally gave up trying to move and, at some point, had passed out.

When dawn broke, the pain hit her like a semitruck. But she was still alive, and the sun doubled her determination to stay that way. In the daylight, she was able to study her surroundings for the first time. How she'd survived that fall, she'd never know. But the jagged rocks in the dry, elevated areas—normally a danger—had proved to be her salvation.

She'd managed to roll herself over onto a sharp rock ledge peeking up from between some roots in the dry dirt. And for the next hour she worked, moving just her wrists until the lime-green kernmantle rope she'd been bound in frayed and split.

The crazy bastard who tied her up and left her for dead wasn't the only one who knew how to climb, who knew about knots and understood a rope's strengths and weaknesses.

By the time Aliyah had broken free, she was crying tears for another reason—joy, however momentary. Though weak, she stood and looked around, trying to calculate her next best move. That was when she spotted another person in her same predicament.

She started to run, and knifelike pain shot through her right hip. She crashed to the hard earth, skinning her knees further. She stayed down and crawled over instead, favoring that leg.

It was her former coworker, Parker Roy, his tanned skin ghost-white, his blond hair a dusty gray. He was deader than dead.

She'd stifled a scream with both hands to her mouth, and that was when she thought she heard a vehicle above. She started crying, choking down sobs in an attempt to stay quiet.

What if the car above was her attacker? What if—

She gasped. What if he had another victim he was tossing over the cliff?

Summoning her inner reserves, she stood through the pain. Tears streamed down her face and onto her white blouse as she scanned the area.

Aliyah took off down the ravine, limping but making good time, despite her hip, her high heels, and her pencil skirt. She cursed herself for wearing her fancy shoes to work —the whole damn outfit—still trying to impress her new bosses.

She'd been in the wilderness fighting for her life for over thirty-six hours now. And she was still cursing those shoes that she kept taking off and putting back on. Her feet were blistered, and her heels had been oozing pus for the last day. But her bare feet on the jagged rocks was even worse.

Aliyah was hardly a forager, but when she moved to Texas for college, she joined the UT Austin Texas Rock Climbing club to make friends. In addition to gaining her mad skills as a climber, the experience was like taking a crash course in geoscience, including some botany. She didn't know about all the plant life she couldn't eat, but she knew what was definitely safe.

She'd been living off berries along with some flowers such as the just-in-bloom dandelions. They were bitter like red wine gone bad but weren't going to kill her, and she was hardly spoiled for choice. Thistles would've been fully edible, but they were not yet in bloom, so she had to make do with gnawing on some roots. Getting pierced by a thousand tiny thistles was the price for this small scrap of nourishment.

Last night, she'd slept under a pile of branches she'd collected to stay warm and hidden.

Not that she'd gotten much sleep.

Travel had been slow for hours, and her pain was getting worse. Plus, with the cuts all over her skin, well, it felt like she was undergoing pinprick torture with every twist and turn. She couldn't imagine her abrasions ever healing. And her spiraling black curls were a mass of twigs, dirt, and sweat.

It was late and so very dark as she worked her way up a rocky hillside. Whenever she took a break to take weight off her hip, she heard all the creatures of the night, taunting her. All she wanted was her down comforter and ergonomic pillow. And yet, she'd give her savings for her ratty old flannel and a bottle of tepid water.

At least her guilt over Christina's death was gone, replaced by determination to get out of the forest alive—to live her life with more presence of mind, more compassion for those around her.

Parker Roy was dead. Her former coworker. That was no coincidence. But the overlapping section of possibilities in the Venn diagram in her mind didn't reveal any answers as to who the killer could be. Still, she was convinced the person who did this was someone she knew.

If this place didn't kill her, if a mountain lion didn't tear her apart and dine on her heart, if that maniac didn't hunt her down and slice her to bits, she was going to come out the other end stronger and make the bastard pay. Her thoughts slushed in her brain, dark and muddy as the starless night sky.

She shuddered at the thought of another night in the woods, but it was late, and she was exhausted. As she spun to find a spot to lie down, her hip gave way.

Her heel slipped on a mossy rock. She lost her footing and went down. Digging her nails into the spongy surface ripped the last of her acrylics off.

Aliyah let out a scream that came out more like a whimper. She whispered a curse after that. She'd been yelling for help sporadically, but she was dehydrated. Her voice was giving out on her, and she needed to preserve it.

Her fingers were tired, her nails bloody, and her grip strength was faltering. One hand lost its hold, then the other, and she began to slide over the slick rocks and moist earth into the utter blackness of a cave system below.

13

The next morning, after checking in with Mullaney and receiving the disappointing news that Aliyah Andry hadn't been recovered from the wilderness preserve yet, Winter reported for her first official day as the newest employee of Cumberland Mountain Equipment.

While her husband had privately approved of her new work attire, he was wary about letting her out the door in it. But he knew better than to try and stand in her way when she was on a mission.

She was expecting a morning of filling out paperwork and trailing Melissa—the somewhat surly veteran employee who seemed to keep all her opinions very close to the vest. Instead, as Winter stepped into the wide atrium, she was greeted by Nathan Lynch himself, who stood near the longest practice wall with ropes and other equipment piled near his feet.

"Good morning, Sam." Nathan smiled. He'd traded out his tailored suit for slim-fit khakis, blue climbing shoes, and a t-shirt that showed off every muscle in his chest. And he had an arm wrapped around a white helmet. "Are you ready for the last part of your interview?"

Her eyes darted between him, the rope, and the wall. "What do you mean?"

"Here at Cumberland, we are so much more than just talk. Every one of us, from the accounting department to the salesforce and even Dawn, our friendly receptionist, are all climbers ready to demonstrate and expertly recommend our products at a moment's notice." He stepped closer until he stood less than two feet from her.

She wanted to step back, get away from the abrasive smell of his cologne.

Flirt with him, Winter. More bees with honey.

It made her literally sick, but she looked up at him shyly from under her lashes. "What do you want me to do?"

"I want to see how high you can climb." He stole another quick glance down her shirt. The barest tip of his tongue brushed the corner of his upper lip. Then his eyes dipped to her feet. "How much mentoring you might need." Then he turned toward the receptionist. "Dawn, grab some shoes from the bin. Size nine."

Dawn was up and out of her seat, a pair of gray-and-teal rock climbing shoes in hand. "Here you go, Sam. Have fun."

Winter kept a blank face and sat on the floor. She swapped out her hiking boots for the climbing shoes, refusing to be impressed by Nathan guessing her shoe size.

"Okay." Winter stood and, diverting all her nervous energy into her hands, reached for the helmet. She glanced up the wall. She'd never actually been to a climbing gym. And before yesterday, the only climbing experience she'd ever had was the wall obstacle in a standard course.

Cumberland's walls were three stories high. Now that she was taking a closer look, she realized even the waterfall wall had handholds and footholds arranged beside it. The ceiling was slightly curved, no hard angles, with a summit where a climber would be forced to cling like a lizard, upside down. From there, at the very center of the ceiling, was a skylight—a sheer shaft a bit like a chimney. No holds, but hanging from the very center was a little red flag.

Did people actually climb all the way up there?

A hand brushed the small of her back. Winter forced down her instinct to break his arm.

"We call that the Summit." Nathan stood at her side, gazing up at the red flag. "If you reach that flag, you get to keep it and wear it with your uniform. It's a token of honor."

She turned to look at him. His face was so close to hers she could've taken a bite right out of his cheek. "You expect me to climb all the way up there?"

He laughed like the self-righteous son of a bitch he clearly was. "Only a handful of us have ever reached the Summit. No girls in that club."

Every muscle in Winter's body twitched with the thinly veiled insult. He had no idea who he was talking to. Still, it was good to know. Anybody who could make that climb would be able to handle the area where Parker Roy, and possibly Aliyah Andry, had been dumped.

"Okay." She sighed and put on the helmet. "I'll do my best. I'm a little rusty."

"Don't worry. I'll tie you up tight." He picked up the harness and helped her into it—an action that was completely unnecessary and just an excuse to get close to her thighs. Then he tied her into the guide rope, threaded it through both hard points on her harness, and finished it off with a trace eight.

It was the first knot Winter had made a point to master—the only one needed to climb in a gym, which was all she was claiming. *First, build a figure eight in the slack before threading up the harness, then follow the track with the working end.*

She watched Nathan's expert hands, deft and flawless. Though she fought to stay calm and present, when she blinked, she was back in the forest with Deputy Mullaney, staring at a blood-tinged twist of knots and a faint red glow.

Though she tried not to, Winter imagined herself in Parker Roy's place. The knots pulling tight. The last sensation he ever felt would've been the burn.

The rope was already threaded through a loop at the top near the shaft in the ceiling. Nathan held the belaying end. His job was to give her enough slack to move and hold her tight should she happen to slip and fall.

And show off his muscles in the meantime, no doubt.

Her life was technically in his hands. From what she'd learned so far about climbing, the belay partnership was one that took time to develop, since so much trust and communication was involved. Not giving enough slack could lead to slips, and giving too much could lead to injury or death. Usually, all a climber had to worry about was their belay partner making an honest mistake.

Unfortunately, Winter's partner was Nathan freaking Lynch.

But she had to trust him, at least in this very narrow bubble of time. And trust in the strength and skill of her own fingers.

She approached the wall, then reached into the chalk bag on the harness to dust her hands. She grasped the first holds and started climbing. Her muscles were tense, aching with all the self-control it took not to spit on him. Knowing he was watching her, looking at her ass.

The harness itched at the bare skin of her legs.

"You climb in pants, you utter prick," she whispered under her breath, now far enough away she knew he would not hear. Arm over arm she climbed. "No wonder no 'girls' can reach the Summit. Fuck you."

"Looking good." The tone in his voice was a lounge lizard talking up a showgirl. "Don't overreach now. One little slip and you'll be dangling at the end of my rope."

"That'll be the day." She made sure to smile over her shoulder. Flirty, not murderous. She reached even higher, kicking off her back foot to catch a hold just beyond her fingertips.

Her disgust with Lynch roused an old feeling, one she didn't suffer much anymore. Back at the academy and early on with the Bureau, she'd suffered her fair share of disgusting men and had always made it a point to show them she was not going to take their shit. She was hardheaded first, a skilled agent second.

But Nathan Lynch was different because she had to take his shit to get what she wanted.

Fortunately, she didn't plan to take his shit for long.

Winter reached the curve that would take her up onto the ceiling, beckoning her to hang underneath it like a lizard from a log.

Maybe there was some fancy rope trick she could've used. If so, Winter didn't know it yet. All she had was brute strength and a total pigheaded unwillingness to let him, Nathan Lynch, beat her in anything ever.

As she pulled herself parallel, her back to the ground, the door swung open, and four men dressed in the same uniform worn by Deputy Mullaney entered the atrium. Officers with the Texas State Park Police, the agency currently working Parker Roy's homicide, all in their tan campaign hats. Was it news about Aliyah Andry?

Does one of them look extra tall?

Focus, Winter!

Lynch glanced over his shoulder, barely seeming to register their presence before turning his attention back to

Winter. He stared at her like she was a five-course meal and he hadn't eaten in weeks.

"Excuse me." One of the rangers approached him. "We're here in regard to the recent homicide of Parker Roy and the subsequent disappearance of Aliyah Andry. We need to speak with Mr. Lynch."

"Yeah. Just a second." He brushed them off, his eyes never leaving her.

Winter's hands began to shake. She'd stayed motionless for too long. Fixing her sights firmly on the goal in front of her, she swung her arm forward and pulled her body up. The soles of her shoes pressed hard into the curved footholds, holding up her weight with her toes.

"You lied to me. You said you couldn't climb!" Nathan laughed.

"We're investigating a homicide," the deputy continued. His voice was muffled, farther away and mixing with the sound of the waterfall.

Winter stole one final glance down. She was so high up with a sheer drop below. And Lynch—though he watched her with rapt attention—had a loose grip on the line.

Fear crept up her spine like walking fingers. Yeah, she got up here on her own, but she was going to need him to get down. At least there were a few of Texas's finest down there. They'd make sure she got down alive.

Noah was not going to like this story. Maybe she wouldn't tell him.

Winter laughed, catching her breath in the friction hold, and glanced up the ten-foot shaft at the tiny red flag hanging above.

"You're tired," Nathan teased, his voice echoing all around her. "You used up all your energy getting there. I'm very proud of you. But there's no shame in giving up."

"Condescending mother..." Winter gritted her teeth to

keep the evil in. Then she raised her voice. "I got energy for days!"

First, she re-chalked her hands, then started walking her feet up the wall, pushing her back up the opposite side like the Grinch going up a chimney. The slabs of rock were solid and moist from the rising mist of the water. She had to pause to wipe the bottoms of her shoes off on her legs, one by one.

The maneuver was simple enough, but slow. One step at a time upward, her thighs burning. She'd used up a lot of energy on the lizard crawl or whatever the hell that was. But she wasn't going to give up.

She slipped, and her shoulders slid down six inches all at once. She had to tighten her knees to stay up. The rush of vertigo hit her again. She pushed it aside, keeping her eyes open. Focused.

He wouldn't let her drop. Not in front of all those cops. He wouldn't.

Inch by inch, she made her way to the top. The flag was a scant yard away.

"All right. I've had enough of this. It's time to get her down," one of the rangers said roughly.

Winter stretched, but the rope of her harness was too tight, holding her back. She lifted her voice to call for slack when there was a pull on the rope, a tug no rougher than a cat pawing at the end of a string. Her foot slipped as she readied to make her final reach. Her shoulder followed.

Winter's stomach lurched as she began to fall. Her limbs shot out, and her fingers scraped along the rock. She had no time wonder in a vague primeval language if she was going to die before the rope caught tight.

Lynch held her up with his muscles pumped, looking like a hero. The flag remained at the top of the atrium.

No girls in the club.

Slowly, Lynch let out the line, lowering her from the ceiling like a limp spider on a string.

When her feet touched the ground, she took one unsteady step before finding balance.

She stayed with her back to him as she crouched and untied the climbing shoes, keeping her head down as Lynch approached her. Out of the corner of her eye, she spotted a ranger on his heels, waiting to question him for homicide. A tall, lanky one.

"You lied to me." Lynch looked down at her, grinning. "You're going to be trouble. I can tell."

Rock climbing shoes hooked in her left hand, Winter turned and reached out with her right toward Deputy Mullaney.

"Sum—"

"Hi, there, I'm Sam Drewitt." She widened her eyes, silently pleading for him to go along. "How are you doing this morning, Deputy?"

"I'm…" He blinked for a moment before shaking her hand. "I'm fine. We're, um, going to need your boss for a few minutes."

An older ranger, mid-fifties, tapped Lynch's shoulder.

At his insistence, Nathan led him and two others toward his office.

Mullaney stayed behind. "We'll need your statement, too, um, Sam."

Nathan was still in earshot when she replied, "I don't know anything. I'm new."

Mullaney arched an eyebrow, and Winter felt like she was staring up at the ironic frown of a young Darnell Davenport.

14

Winter spent the rest of the morning in the office with Melissa pretending to care about filing systems, computer applications, and other workplace details that went through Winter's brain like water through a colander. She tried to hold on, but her mind was buzzing with a thousand different songs. Nathan and the rope and Parker Roy and Aliyah Andry and the police.

She needed to make sure she and the investigators were on the same page, but at the same time, she didn't want any bad acting on the part of the park rangers to give her away.

She felt like she'd won Mullaney over for the second time, but that didn't mean it would stick.

A little before lunch, as Winter worked on some filing Melissa had given her, she took advantage of the silence for her first attempt at friendly conversation. "So how long have you worked here, Melissa?"

She gave an audible sigh. "I dunno. Six. Seven…holy crap. Nine years."

"So you must know everything there is to know about Cumberland."

"Nine years." She clicked her mouse rather hard a few times, then turned to Winter. "Look, you seem like a nice girl. I hope you know what you're getting into."

"What do you mean?"

"I mean, this is a great job. Great benefits. Vacation. I get to go on climbing holidays all over the world."

"Really?" Helen hadn't mentioned that.

"Yeah, Nathan sponsors at least two trips a year. Last time, we went to the red rocks in Utah. It was amazing." Her words were pleasant, but her expression suggested somebody had just asked her to give a eulogy. "He gets this big house, and we stay together. Like a team-building activity."

A knock came at the door, startling her. Helen poked her head in with a ghost of a smile. "Nathan wants us all in the conference room."

"Is this about Parker?" Melissa asked.

Helen nodded, eyes downcast, and then slipped away.

Melissa turned to Winter. "Somebody tied him up and left him at the bottom of a canyon to choke himself to death." Her eyes almost glistened as she spoke, no hint of sympathy.

"That's terrible. Do they know who did it?"

"They think one of us did, obviously. Especially now that Aliyah's gone missing too."

"Who's Aliyah?"

Melissa stood, brushing out invisible wrinkles from her tight skirt. "Just another person who used to work here. Seems like quite a coincidence to me."

They came into the room while Nathan was already addressing the team. "It's imperative that everyone fully cooperates with the investigation. We need to do everything we can to make it easy for the police to see what's going on here and protect us. There are no suspects in Parker's murder from what I understand."

Maybe the police don't have a suspect yet, but I know I do.

"They think somebody might be stalking the building, so we're going to be tightening security. We all have our little key fobs, but I know we get lazy and leave doors open. No more. Everyone in and out needs to be logged into our system. Sales team, this includes customers. You need to set and keep appointments and make sure the name of every guest is logged, including the time they arrived and the time they left."

"Are they saying he was murdered here in the building?" Winter whispered to Melissa.

"Are they saying he was murdered here in the building?" Melissa asked her CEO.

Good girl, Melissa.

"They're saying it's possible Parker might have been on the premises when he was initially abducted. Which is why I'm also instituting a buddy policy. Nobody goes into that parking lot alone. When you come in to work, call somebody inside the building to come out and meet you before you exit your car. If you have to work late, I'm usually here, especially these days. Don't be shy to come to my office, and I'll escort you to your vehicle myself."

Melissa's eyeroll was practically audible. Across the room, Winter met Helen's frightened owl eyes.

"What happened to Aliyah?" Winter asked.

Lynch's eyes turned to her, intense and probing. Undressing her in front of everyone.

"The police didn't have much to say about that other than the investigation is ongoing. There's still a strong chance the two crimes are unrelated. Our thoughts and prayers are with her family, but there's not much we can do other than let the authorities do their jobs. This is highly unusual, Sam. So, well, let's all keep trying to do our jobs 'til this blows over."

He clapped his hands, dismissing any further questions. "Now gear up, and let's go."

15

Noah sat in his truck in the parking lot of the Cumberland offices, waiting for Winter to take her lunch break. His collar was itchy. He'd checked himself last night in the shower and found a weird rash snaking over his shoulders and down his spine. He didn't know what the hell it was, but as he ruminated about Winter in this place, all alone, and telling him to keep his big nose out of it, it itched even more.

He unzipped the duffel bag at his side and fiddled with some little black disks he'd brought along to give to his wife. State-of-the-art concealed listening devices she could mount on desks, coffee makers, conference tables, anywhere an important conversation might be taking place. He'd even brought one for her to wear, so anything she happened to finesse out of these people could be catalogued and possibly used as evidence.

Winter might be resistant to the idea, but he'd come here today with his determination screwed to the sticking point. If he couldn't join her in the lion's den, the least she could do was give him a fighting chance of coming to her rescue should anything go south.

After all, they weren't just dealing with your average predatory douche in a suit. Nathan Lynch could very well be a murderer with a bondage fixation and a strong preference for beautiful, athletic women. And Winter was in there with him. All alone.

Noah shook his head to try to clear out the smoky nightmares forming in his mind's eye. He'd do whatever it took to convince Winter to wear the audio recorder. And he wasn't above deploying full puppy dog eyes to get his way.

His phone rang, and he checked the ID. Gramma Beth.

He smiled and swiped to answer. "Well good afternoon, young lady."

"Hi, Noah. Sorry if I'm catching you at work."

"No problem at all." It occurred to him to tell her about his leave, but any version of the words *I don't technically have a job right now* caught in his throat like tacks. "To what do I owe the pleasure?"

"I don't suppose you're anywhere near Winter?"

"So close but so far. She's got a big case going on right now."

"I figured." Winter's loving grandmother managed to sound both profoundly proud and concerned in just two little words.

He knew exactly how she was feeling.

"I haven't been able to get her on the phone the last little while. Could you please let her know to call me when she has a chance?"

"Will do. She's been in places where she can't exactly have her phone on her."

"The less I know about it the better. I'm just worried about her, that's all."

You and me both.

"I understand. I'll be sure to get her on the horn this evening."

"Thanks. I won't take up too much of your time. I know you're a busy man."

"Yes…" He looked down at the duffel bag, at the radio he'd been zoning out to for the last two hours. "Very busy."

"Talk to you later." Gramma Beth hung up. Noah lowered his phone and gazed at the lock screen—a photo of Winter with her ice-blue eyes, long black hair, and snow-white skin. She was so beautiful. *Watch her from across the room* kind of beautiful. *Become obsessed with her from a single glance* kind of beautiful.

He checked the time. Ten minutes 'til her scheduled lunch break. Then he rubbed his back against the seat, scratching the flare of stinging itchiness running down his vertebrae.

❄

After Nathan's speech, Winter had followed Melissa back to the office to finish up the filing before clocking off for her lunch break. Even a half day of being a regular employee had reminded her why she'd decided to work for herself. Being a grunt was exhausting.

Or maybe it was the rock wall that was exhausting.

Her loosened muscles ached in the most pleasant possible way. As much as she tried to put it out of her mind, that little red flag still hanging from the ceiling atrium distracted her.

No girls in the club.

Winter couldn't remember the last time she'd wanted to wallop another human being quite as much as Nathan Lynch.

She kept chewing on the way he watched her even as the rangers wanted to question him about a homicide. He was fixated, a state that reeked of obsession.

Had he ever looked at Christina Norris like that? She could imagine how it might've affected someone like her—

someone who, if Helen was to be believed, was the very definition of an ingenue.

A man cleared his throat.

Winter tensed and turned to see Lieutenant Fafa Jallow of the National Park Service standing in the doorway. She didn't know him well, as they had never worked together. But they ran in similar circles and had chatted at the police officers' ball last year about their mutual disdain for overly sweet, dry-crumb cupcakes as they helped themselves to seconds.

He was in his early forties. Tall and muscular with smooth, nearly black skin and sharp, angular features. His cheekbones alone could cut glass. Jallow was a unique kind of handsome. A face that was impossible to forget. And, of course, that white hat.

For her part, Winter hoped she hadn't been as memorable.

He introduced himself quickly, flashing his badge. "Which one of you is Melissa Hinds?"

"That's me." For the first time since Winter had met the woman, Melissa had what looked like a genuine smile on her face. She rose from her desk and moved toward Jallow, more floating than walking. "What can I do for you, Detective?"

Apparently, Melissa had also taken note of Jallow's indisputable handsomeness.

"Lieutenant Jallow," he said smoothly. "And I was hoping I could ask you a couple of questions, Mrs. Hinds."

"Miss," she corrected, swift as a bullet. "And you can call me Melissa."

"Melissa." Jallow smiled, showing a row of bright-white teeth. Winter kept her head down, trying to make her exit.

"I'm sorry. Could I have your name, please?"

Winter clenched her teeth. He wouldn't be stupid enough to out her even if he did recognize her. Would he?

"That's just Sam," Melissa answered for her. "She's brand new. She doesn't know anything. She never even met Parker. I, on the other hand, can tell you anything you want to know."

"And we appreciate your cooperation."

Winter saw her chance and slipped by Jallow. It was time for lunch anyway. Unfortunately, as she moved down the hall, Nathan turned a corner and nearly chest-bumped her.

His eyes locked onto hers. "Hello, Sam."

"Hi." She forced herself to smile shyly, then wound a strand of her hair around a finger and fiddled with it.

"That was very impressive this morning. I wish we hadn't been interrupted. I'm just, well, I wasn't expecting it. You've surprised me."

"Thank you." She glanced off to one side. "Is everything all right? You seem distracted."

"You're perceptive too. You remind me of…" He stopped, staring past her at seemingly nothing.

Was Nathan about to cry? He looked lost in space. "I remind you of who, Nathan?"

He visibly shook off whatever it was he was thinking about. "Never mind. You okay?"

She forced a shiver. "All this stuff with the cops has me a little spooked."

Nathan set his hand on her shoulder and lowered his voice. "You have nothing to worry about. It's my personal mission to protect every soul in this building." He heaved out a sigh.

"Okay, um, thank you."

"Were you about to take your lunch break?"

She had the horrible suspicion that he was about to insist on walking her to her car when a peal of laughter rang through the hall. His head snapped up, and his ears practically pricked as the banter between Jallow and Melissa drifted over them. The tone sounded nothing like a somber interview about the grisly death of a coworker. It sounded more like cocktail hour.

"Who's in there with her?" The emotion had left his voice.

"One of the rangers. He wanted to interview her—"

"Leave it to Melissa to flirt with the fucking cops." His grip tightened on her shoulder. It wasn't quite painful, but it was noticeable enough that she had to suppress her urge to shake him off.

Winter was genuinely taken aback by his outburst. She'd taken him as having more control over himself than that. "What's the harm in a little flirting? She's not interfering or anything."

"I don't tolerate office liaisons. And I'm certainly not going to tolerate Melissa's incessant…" He cut himself off and cracked his neck, perhaps recognizing how he might be appearing to her. "Cool it, Nate buddy."

Did he just…talk to himself?

"Will you excuse me, please?" At last, he lifted his hand from Winter's shoulder and marched down the hall into Melissa's office.

She shook off the cringe left behind by his touch and was about to resume her best attempt at evasive action when she noticed Nathan Lynch's assistant, Bryan Green, coming out of the copy room, a stack of papers in his hands.

Christina's boyfriend.

Winter hadn't had a chance to talk to him yet. Like all the men she'd seen at Cumberland, Bryan had an athletic build. He was an attractive, dark-haired man—but one look was all it took to see the pain hiding in plain sight. The loss he'd experienced.

Bryan walked up to her. "Are you okay?"

That caught her off guard. "I'm fine. What do you mean?"

"Nathan has a bad temper. That was nothing. When he gets like that, it's best to stay out of his way." He stepped past her. He couldn't have been more different than his boss. Shy and reserved, he took every care to keep from accidentally brushing Winter as he passed.

"You're Bryan, right?" Winter followed him with her eyes.

"Mm-hmm."

"Sam." She put out her hand, and he shook it. Not too soft, but not too firm. A perfectly respectable handshake. And when it was done, he retreated back another few inches.

"I heard what happened to your girlfriend," she said, knowing it was a gamble. "I'm so, so sorry. I know what it's like to lose somebody like that."

He looked down, hugging the papers a little tighter to his chest. His Adam's apple bounced as he swallowed. "Yeah."

"It's horrible, and nothing anybody can say can make it better."

Bryan's face tightened. Then he lifted his eyes shyly. They were so flat, almost empty. Like he'd spent the last two weeks crying out his very life force. The expression tugged hard on Winter's heart.

He nodded, then without another word, continued down the hallway.

As she made her way out of the building and took a much-needed gasp of sunlight-soaked fresh air, she pulled out her phone and checked her notifications. A stream of texts from Ranger Deputy Mullaney pulled her gaze.

I've got some interesting results back on the ropes you found.
Do you eat food?
I'll be having lunch at one o'clock at Brew and Grind on Sunnyvale.

Winter glanced at the time. Twelve thirty. She and Noah could make it if they sped.

Lifting her gaze to see him and his big Beulah in the lot brought a smile to her cheeks. If she'd needed to be on the moon by one o'clock, Noah was exactly the person she would ask to drive her there.

16

What the hell happened to Aliyah's corpse?

They'd found Parker's remains. I knew they would, though it happened sooner than I anticipated. But I never imagined they'd only find one body. There were two down there.

Two! What the hell?!

Just calm the fuck down, man.

There was no way she could have survived. Surely, she was just carried off by coyotes. By now, she was mush, digesting in some canid's stomach.

That had to be it. Wild dogs ravaged her.

Or my rig failed again, still imperfect. Maybe that was it. Still not doing the job I designed it to do. Maybe I'd been using the wrong kind of rope. Maybe in a search for finesse, I'd given up too much strength. Next time, I'd try out a nine and a half millimeter kernmantle.

Leave it to Aliyah to ruin everything. As usual.

I snatched a half rope from the bin near my desk and tied a trace eight. A soothing knot, my favorite. "Follow the track, caress the line…"

I heard the cackle of the herd and peeked out from my office to see Helen and Melissa standing down the hall, doing nothing. Over-tanned Melissa, not even taking a police investigation seriously. Helen still had a bit of glow about her.

"Follow the track and double back..."

I liked those big, innocent eyes of Helen's. But she wasn't. Innocent. She was exactly the same as the others. The same as Aliyah and Parker. The same as Melissa and Tucker.

They closed their eyes and their hearts as they patiently waited for you to succumb.

The new girl might be different, though. Her cold blue eyes were soothing, like gazing into a quiet blizzard. I wondered where she'd gone and when she'd be back.

If she'd left the building, she hadn't used the buddy system as instructed.

Melissa looked over at me and stared. I wasn't in the mood for her, not today.

My hands fumbled on my knot as I retreated into the office. I traced the eight repeatedly and ran out of line. It was useless now—swollen and tangled.

"Filthy, no-good hunk of shit!" I threw it across the room where it hit the wall with a heavy thud.

My father used to say that to me. I told you once how he'd treat me, and you touched my cheek with your silky hand, tears in your eyes. Tears for me that I wanted to see you shed. God, you were beautiful when you cried. Like dew on a spider's web.

Aliyah might've gotten off easy. If she was still alive, would it really matter? She never saw my face. Not even my skin. She barely saw me at all.

She doesn't know who I am.

But what if she recognized my voice? Or my smell? Or...?

I couldn't risk it. If they caught me, they'd kill me. Eventually. Somehow. Aliyah better be dead.

If not, when I find her, she's going to suffer for the trouble she's caused me.

I dropped the rope and began to pace my office. I felt so tight, like bolts of electricity were striking every bone. I wanted to get away from the police and the cackling whores. Out into nature. But it seemed a waste of a trip to go alone.

Just then, I heard that voice near my door. Melissa, flicking her hair again. Laughing again and teasing. Who was it now? The cop had left.

I could just grab her right now, pull her in here. Tie her up. Choke her like her many lovers had, but harder and harder, watching the fear grow in her eyes as she realized I was never going to let go. The ropes squeezing tighter on her naked body, knots burrowing into her flesh. Her hips, her ribs, her breasts.

I was beginning to twitch as I peered out of my door. Oh, it was Tucker Hicks who was with Melissa now. The poser. The wannabe. Every word that came out of his ass-kissing mouth was worse than excrement.

"There's my gorgeous little moneymaker." Tucker laced a hand on Melissa's waist. She pirouetted, smiling and dipping to give him and me and everyone else another view of her fake tits.

"Oh, go on, you." Her lips brushed his cheek. As they passed one another, their little dance at an end, Tucker slapped her ass for good measure.

The sound it made was exquisite. Like a steel line being pulled taut.

And of course, ever the coquette, Melissa pursed her lips and played innocent, even as she shook her ass with every step down the hall.

My eyes followed the sway of her hips until she was gone, then I returned to Tucker.

His little moneymaker, hmm?

Tucker hadn't helped either. If he'd acted right all along, maybe none of this ever would've happened. I'd been saving him as part of my grand finale…but I could always move him up on my list.

Somebody was coming with me to the woods. The great whore or the lying sycophant. Both excellent choices.

You and I both know what needs to happen next.

17

Winter smiled when Noah made record time to Brew and Grind. She filled him in on what happened at Cumberland while waiting for Deputy Mullaney to show, glossing over the intense interactions she'd had with Nathan Lynch. And the whole *might have literally put her life in the hands of a killer* thing.

He looked a bit stressed. She'd bring it up later.

When Mullaney arrived, he poked his head about in the air like a flamingo, then waved when he spotted her. As he sat down, he looked genuinely pleased she'd showed. Like a middle schooler who'd talked the hot girl into sitting with him at lunch.

"Deputy Mullaney, this is my husband, Special Agent Noah Dalton."

"Wow. Yes. Hi." He smiled and shook Noah's hand. "Call me Lyle."

"Nice to meet you, Lyle." Noah leaned back in his seat, his arm thrown over the back of the booth. Casual dominant positioning.

Winter nursed her oversize mocha. "So looks like the investigation is coming along…"

"Just as we thought, those small, narrow tracks at the scene are consistent with Aliyah Andry's shoe size. We lost the tracks at a stream, though, and search efforts have been unsuccessful. But we were able to get DNA from the blood spatter of the potential second victim. Should be ready soon. I found Aliyah Andry's DNA too. Looks like she did one of those genealogy tests a while back."

Winter bristled. Hopefully, Aliyah's DNA was put there by Aliyah. Those websites were useful in her line of work, though she'd yet to make peace with them.

"So about you now, *Sam*…"

"Yes, okay, I've gone undercover at Cumberland. You know I'm a P.I. Thanks for not blowing my cover."

"Do you think that's safe?"

Noah pushed his sunglasses down to the tip of his nose and looked over them at her, saying everything without saying a word.

"There are always risks inherent with going undercover." She returned the gaze with a dead-faced glare until he pushed the glasses back up. "An employee of Cumberland hired me to look into possible misconduct by the CEO, which they claim was ignored by HR. In my research, I found Parker Roy had filed suit against both Cumberland and Nathan Lynch personally, seeking damages for being subjected to a hostile work environment."

"Maybe…" Lyle drummed his fingers on the table. "But he has a solid alibi for the night of the murders."

"I gotta hear this."

"He was at home with his wife and kids. Then he called to check on his father, confirmed by the record, at around nine o'clock. Went to bed early."

She'd nearly forgotten Lynch was a married man with children. It made her want to take a scalding shower.

"Wives lie for their husbands."

"True enough, but he also lives in a gated community with a security guard who keeps track of every person and vehicle that goes in or out. Says Lynch never left the subdivision."

Winter balled a fist. Noah set his hand lightly on her knee under the table.

She put her hand on top of his and squeezed. "How long has Parker Roy been dead? And Aliyah Andry hasn't been found. You can't have accounted for Lynch's whereabouts all week."

Mullaney shook his head. "Yeah, you're right. The timelines aren't rock-solid."

Winter hadn't meant to deflate the young officer. She knew how hard he was working.

"Besides," he went on, "the wheels on Lynch's Tesla Model Y do not remotely match the tracks we found. Which are Michelin Defender XTS, by the way."

Winter brightened. "How different are they?"

"They're used for heavy off-roading. Pretty common tires among folks who do a lot of hunting or camping. But they're not especially common with the general population. We're compiling a list of purchases in a three-hundred-mile radius going back the last few years, but it'll take time."

"That's good news. Good work." With a final squeeze, Winter let go of her husband's hand and clasped both of hers around her bowl-sized mug once again. "Tell me more about the knots."

"Yeah, the knots." Lyle took out his phone and poked around a bit before reading aloud. "The rope was nine-millimeter static climbing rope, color lime green. The brand is carried by Cumberland and other retailers. Fairly common, unfortunately. Still, the climbing community isn't huge, so we're working on tracking down purchases."

"Okay…" More evidence that the killer was probably someone Parker Roy knew. A few minutes ago, Winter had been almost positive that Lyle was going to relay information damning Nathan Lynch. Truth was, though she knew it was important to always keep an open mind, she wasn't ready to give up on him as a suspect.

"Are you gonna share with the group?" Noah could always tell when the wheels in her head were spinning.

"I'm just wondering…" She tapped her finger on the side of her mug. "Maybe, in spite of his carefully cultivated image of ruggedness, Nathan Lynch doesn't actually like to get his hands dirty."

"You mean a hired kill?"

The question was like touching a pin to a delicate bubble. "No, probably not. I'd more likely see him as someone with an accomplice. Maybe somebody lower than him who could benefit from having Lynch on his side."

Tucker Hicks came to mind. The twisted HR manager who had all of Lynch's slimiest qualities and none of his effortless charm.

"There's still something I'm not seeing." Winter turned back to Lyle. "Have you consulted with the FBI on this?"

"No. I feel like the park rangers have this handled."

"Yeah. FBI, CIA, Parks and Rec…" Noah dipped his head from side to side. "Those things are comparable."

Now it was Winter's turn to put her hand on his knee.

Lyle gave a little grin, as if to acknowledge Noah's point. "Well, it's one victim and one missing person, and Search and Rescue's all over it. That's what I meant."

Noah relaxed a little under her grip.

"I'm canvassing equipment stores for the rope this afternoon," Lyle said. "I'll let you know if I find anything."

"Thank you. I appreciate it." Winter smiled.

"I still worry about you getting into bed with Cumberland. Our leading theory is that the killer works there."

"From my perspective, I'm the safest person in that office." Winter glanced out the window, images of Helen and Melissa, of Bryan and Dawn, floating behind her eyes. "It's everybody else I'm worried about."

18

Tucker Hicks had always prided himself on being a logical man. With all this police attention around Cumberland now, he knew the party was effectively over. It had been good while it lasted. Great at times, even. Having Nathan Lynch for a boss was a blessing. Yeah, the guy thought the sun shined out his own ass, but the truth was, it kind of did.

Up until about four hours ago, Tucker would've paid his last dime to switch places with Lynch. It wasn't just that Lynch was born with a silver spoon in his mouth. Or that his wife was even richer than his daddy, effectively making his continued presence in the workforce a simple matter of pride.

And it wasn't Lynch's position and prestige, nor his charm and good looks. Not only those things. What Tucker admired most about Lynch was his confidence. He was the sort of man who could sell anyone a bridge in Brooklyn. He could land any woman he wanted just by being Nathan Lynch.

The man was a lion—the undisputed king of this jungle. Tucker was a happy turkey vulture. Underrated, but clever animals. Turkey vultures knew how much easier it was to just stand back, let the big guy roar, and clear the path, then swoop in after and pick off the leftovers.

Speaking of…

Tucker took out his phone and texted Melissa. *Dinner is on you tonight, baby. I'll pay for it, of course.*

He chuckled and hit send.

The party was nearly over. Though Cumberland was expanding, they might easily end up getting sued into oblivion. He could smell the friction in the air. Not to mention see the cops in the building. And he was ready to jump ship. Tucker never ceased to keep his résumé up to date and searchable for that very reason.

"Sorry, bro." Tucker kissed two fingers and flicked them at the ceiling. He hated to see it end. Cumberland had been good to him, and not just to his bank account. *And that piece of snow-white ass you just hired…I mean, damn.* It was a shame he wasn't going to get to hit that.

He slapped his desk and laughed nervously, backing away from the proverbial cliff. Maybe Lynch *was* killing people. He could buy it. But even if his boss wasn't a murderer, the cops were bound to find out about all the fucked-up shit around the office. Eventually, they'd look at him, and if he was anything other than squeaky clean…

It's gonna be my ass that gets fed to the wolves.

He ran a hand over his face, wiping away sweat and negative thoughts. Still, they lingered. It wasn't just anxiety about potentially being accused of a few sex crimes. It was grief. A sense of loss over the end of an era.

Tucker was smart enough to appreciate how special Cumberland was. The chances of him finding another gig where he spent half his days flirting with hot women who felt compelled to flirt back…they seemed slim. Yeah, there were climbing gyms and collegial outdoor rec departments—

places he'd have a chance to interact with a lot of young, athletic women. But Tucker couldn't stomach the inevitable pay cut.

Maybe a part-time gig on the side…

Either way, he was determined to ride the Cumberland wave as long as he could, then hop off right before it hit the shore.

He needed to talk to Lynch. See if he could find out the truth—the actual depths of Lynch's crimes. His boss was unstable, emotionally volatile, a spoiled child who thought the entire world belonged to him, and he could sort of believe he was a murderer to boot. He wasn't sure how he felt about that.

Then again, the person Lynch had possibly killed…was Parker Roy.

Tucker wasn't going to waste crocodile tears on that douche canoe. He was a greedy little prick who crashed the party bus without an official invite. What loss was it, really, to have one less Parker Roy in the world?

Maybe he would tell his boss that. Gain his trust. Tell him how he would've killed Roy, too, given the chance. That wasn't true, because Tucker wasn't stupid enough to risk death row over such a pointless little prick. But he could sincerely say that if he saw Roy lying dead in the street, he'd use his back to wipe dogshit off his boot.

Or, if he could gain his boss's trust and get him to confess, he could then turn him over to the police in exchange for immunity for any of Lynch's crimes in which he might have been complicit. Like the cameras in the ladies' restroom, for example.

Tucker took out his phone and texted Melissa three emojis—a peach, a tongue, and fat drops of water.

"It's on, baby. You don't even know."

Then he looked around his office. He was going to miss

Cumberland, one day. But today, all he wanted was to clock out early. He wanted to get home and take a shower before he hooked up with Melissa.

Tucker gathered his things just as there was a knock on his office door.

"Dammit," he muttered. He was almost out of here. "Dickweed. Where would this place be without me?" He huffed to himself.

Jerking the door open he started to ask, "What'd you—"

But he never got his question out. Something snapped against his windpipe so hard, his vision went white. Panic raced through him faster than his thoughts.

A rope. A rope around his neck. His hands shot to it, fighting to get fingers underneath. His assailant shoved him back and kicked the door closed. As Tucker was dragged farther into the office by his neck, he scrambled to get his balance.

He swung his arms wildly, trying to hit his attacker anywhere.

A sharp tug on the rope—the snap of a hangman's noose—and his feet went out from under him. Tucker kicked and struggled.

No air. His vision turned whiter. So tight. Was he bleeding? Fire burned in his chest.

The last thing he saw, before everything was lost, was a hand gloved in black leather coming down on his face.

19

After much convincing, Noah had finally felt comfortable enough to leave Winter at her "new place of work." Unfortunately, the greasy fat cats at Cumberland were not the only threat facing her.

The next day, he made his way to the downtown offices of Black Investigations after an early run and some breakfast. When he stepped in, Ariel was at her little dark-oak reception desk tapping away at her pastel-pink keyboard. Seemed her PC had come back clear of spyware. She tossed him one of her patented smiles, which he answered with a polite nod.

Near the back in Winter's own windowed office—the privacy blinds open—Kline stood on a stool just inside the door.

Noah grumbled. The old bugger had been stabbed in the hand less than a week ago. He was supposed to be taking it easy, not securing crown molding.

"What are you doing?" Noah leaned on the doorframe.

Kline glanced over his shoulder. "Oh, just trying to clean these up. I hate to leave things unfinished once I start them."

That seemed a bit rich, coming from a man who was currently using a dead guy's name, one he found dead in the road. John Drewitt couldn't even finish his own life.

Noah took a deep breath and sighed it out. Like it or not, Kline meant something to Winter. She'd made that clear, once again, last night when she'd told him about how Kline stumbled upon his new identity. And he was her biological father, after all, which meant it was Noah's responsibility to treat him with respect. And to babysit him so he didn't fall and break his neck while healing from a nasty wound. But using a deceased person's identity was fraud. A crime they were both duty bound to report. It wasn't murder, but still…

Noah looked up at Kline, shaking his head. "Get down from there before you hurt yourself."

"I'm not just going to sit around and do nothing." Kline huffed, hammering down another tiny finishing nail. "You and Winter have done everything for me, none of which I've deserved."

Noah drummed his stubby nails against the doorjamb. "There's another way you can help her. A better way."

Finally, the incessant hammering paused. "I'm listening."

"I'm taking a little sabbatical from work for the next few weeks. I got some home reno projects I've been meaning to finish up, but there's something else I need to get to the bottom of first."

Kline lifted his gray eyebrows curiously. It wasn't often Noah could spot any family resemblance between them. Winter was so incredible, and Kline was so ordinary. But he recognized that expression like an old friend.

"You know someone's been stalking Winter. Recording her. Sending her messages. Impersonating her on the internet."

Kline lowered the hammer and slipped it through a loop

on his carpenter's jeans. He stepped down from his little step ladder. "It's Justin. Mark my words."

Noah flinched inwardly at the sound of the vilest name in the English language. "Justin's locked up in supermax. There's no way."

"Justin's cult of personality, then. He has followers. People who'd do anything he said."

Rolling his shoulders to get out the tingles, Noah had no choice but to nod in agreement. "It's not impossible. All the more reason we need to find out who this bastard is and shut him down."

"Okay. I'm game. Where do we start?"

Noah glanced over his shoulder at Ariel, who was typing away at her desk. She had earbuds in, listening to music.

"I don't know how much Winter's said to Ariel about this, but it might be a good idea to keep it mum. Don't wanna scare her for no reason."

Kline nodded, his own gaze sliding toward the young woman. "She's a blabbermouth. Best not to tell her anything about anything, in my opinion."

"In my opinion, your opinion doesn't hold a hell of a lot of weight around here."

"Even after everything that happened, you still don't trust me."

It was a statement, not a question. Still, Noah answered it with a nod.

Kline had saved Winter from being executed, right outside this very building. That, and Winter's own insistence, were the only reasons Noah was willing to put up with him. For the time being.

After all, how could someone using a dead man's name ever be trusted? Living a lie every day, a literal skeleton in their closet.

Kline Hurst—John Drewitt—was capable of anything in

Noah's eyes. The rash on his back flared. Noah threw his right arm over his left shoulder and scratched.

Kline wrinkled his nose. "Whatsa matter with you?"

"I'm fine." He dropped his hand and nestled deeper into his own collar. "I say there's a good chance there's more cameras positioned near the office."

Kline leaned in closer, narrowing his eyes at Noah's neck. "Jesus. You fall in poison oak or something?"

Noah ignored that. "Ready for an Easter egg hunt?"

Kline shrugged, then nodded.

Together, they walked past Ariel, who eyed them suspiciously as they left the building.

Once outside, they separated to scan the streets for cameras. Kline circled around to the narrow back alley while Noah took slow, deliberate steps up and down the sidewalk, his eyes taking in the space. The air was warmer than it had been in weeks, true spring brightening the sky.

Flowering dogwoods across the street were dotted with tiny white buds getting ready to bloom in a few days. The dress shop just down the way had opened its doors, and two racks of clothes were out on the sidewalk to lure in customers. The rains were letting up, heat settling in. Mourning doves cooed from their perches on overhead phone lines.

Noah had walked up and down these streets dozens of times and had taken many jogs through the neighborhood. He pored over his memories—photographs in his mind—and searched for differences. Other than the spring blooms, what had changed in the last few weeks or months?

A few yellow flags no bigger than his palm had been driven into the dirt that lined the easement, marking out gas lines. A new fabric awning was installed over a lawyer's office down the road, a deeper and richer blue than the old one. A lost dog sign was stapled to a telephone pole. And a tiny black nub clung to the pole, just above eye level.

Noah focused on the dab of black, his vision tunneling so he saw nothing else. With a quick glance in either direction, he crossed the street toward it.

A camera. Battery operated. No bigger than a quarter.

His first instinct was to rip it off the pole and smash it to pieces under the heel of his boot. But that wouldn't help him find all the others he had no doubt were out here. And it wouldn't help him find the person responsible for putting them up.

Noah took out his phone and opened an app he often used in his work with the FBI. It was a fair bet this thing was connected to Wi-Fi, uploading what it captured to a cloud for remote viewing. And that meant Noah might be able to pick up its IP address.

The app did its thing—scanning, working, calibrating— and then shot out an answer in the form of a string of numbers and a dot on a minimalistic map. All Noah had to do then was figure out the address of the building the dot belonged to, which was just a matter of plugging latitude and longitude coordinates into another app.

The Duncan Brothers coffee shop just down the road.

"Find something?" Kline asked, stepping up behind him.

Noah nodded, stepping back from the camera. "You ever go to Duncan Brothers down here?"

"No. I know Winter always makes the extra walk to go to a different coffee shop."

"Time for a little road trip." Noah rolled his neck from side to side. "You in?"

"Of course. But why don't we just walk? It's right there."

"Because, genius, I want to stake the place out. Beulah's a lot more comfortable."

Kline nodded, seemingly satisfied.

Together, they crossed the street. Noah was about to peek into the office to let Ariel know they were leaving when he noticed the sign on the door.

Out to lunch. Back by two.

Ariel must've slipped out while he was looking at the camera. No matter. Noah tried the office door just to double-check it was locked, then he and Kline headed to his truck. When he fired it up, he made a point to circle the block, then came back and parked in the lot across the street, positioning the truck so he could see the front door and into a good portion of the shop's transparent windows.

It wasn't the most popular location. As he pulled up, he only noticed a few customers—a woman on her laptop, two men chatting on a sofa. A third man sat by himself at a table, a pinkish drink in front of him. He wore thick glasses and, though he only seemed to be in his early twenties, his hairline was receding. He was dressed in a faded Metallica t-shirt.

To Noah's surprise, a woman he very much recognized walked up from the sidewalk and slipped inside, her brown curls bouncing with every step.

"Ariel…" Noah leaned forward, his eyes glued to her as she greeted the man in the glasses. Then she went to the counter and placed an order before sitting down at the table with him.

Her back was to the window. Noah couldn't see her face.

"Could be a date," Kline said.

"I guess." It really wasn't much of a coincidence that Ariel would come to this place. It was right by her work, after all. And it might not mean much that the camera was connected to the coffee shop's Wi-Fi. Again, proximity. But that didn't stop Noah's nose from twitching. Something off was happening here. That man, Ariel, the camera…

They talked for a long time. The man in the glasses

looked intense, with never a hint of a smile. And he was on his laptop the whole time, jotting down everything Ariel was saying as if he were interviewing her.

"On the other hand," Kline leaned closer to the dashboard, "maybe she's a traitor."

Nearly an hour passed before Ariel left the shop and headed on foot back toward the office.

The man in the glasses stopped to use the restroom, then walked out to his own car—a nondescript, midsize sedan in charcoal gray.

Before he pulled away, Noah jotted down the plates. He texted them to Eve—his partner in the FBI—with a note. *Can you run this for me?*

Not five seconds later, his phone began to ring.

"Noah…"

"Hey."

"You're on leave. What do you need to run a plate for?"

"Oh, you know."

"Winter?"

"Not exactly."

Eve groaned. "You can't keep doing this. I don't want to lose my job, okay?"

"You won't lose your job over one little plate."

"I don't think you fully appreciate just how irritated Falkner is with you right now."

"No, I think I do."

"I'm sorry. I just can't—"

"Please? Just this one. Then I won't ask you for anything else."

"Why you lying?" She heaved a sigh, silence washing into the space between. "Fine. But this is it. I swear to god."

"You're the literal best. Did I ever tell you that?"

"Not nearly often enough." The click of her keyboard, like

the patter of heavy rain, filled the space between them. Eve was one hell of a fast typist. "Carl Gardner."

"You got his ID in front of you?"

"Yeah. Kinda goofy kid with chunky glasses."

"That's the guy. Can you get me an address?"

"All I got on file is his work. A computer repair and tech support company working out of offices out in the industrial district."

"Text it to me."

"All right, cowboy. But when you get yourself brought up on espionage charges, leave my name out of it." Eve hung up. A second later, her text came through. An address complete with zip code. He could just click it, and the phone would lead him right there.

"Stay here." Noah didn't wait for Kline's answer before popping open the door and stepping out. He made his way over to the coffee shop, the smell of the grinding beans wafting through the air. He stepped inside, up to the counter, and got the attention of the barista.

Without thinking much about it, his hand reached for his badge. Technically, he shouldn't be using it at all. But it made opening doors and getting answers just so much easier.

One little flash, one little white lie. It wasn't like the barista would turn him in to Falkner.

The barista's gaze flicked from the badge to Noah's face. Noah's mouth curved up. "Excuse me. My name is Special Agent Noah Dalton with the FBI. I need to speak with the owner about your security setup."

20

On her third day at Cumberland, just after lunch, Winter made a point to visit Helen. Instead of talking in her office, they sat down together at a picnic table in the central courtyard, which was flanked with smaller bouldering walls for employees to enjoy some exercise and sunshine. But the pair of them were alone.

"Okay, so—" Winter had a list of questions she'd been wanting to ask, but the woman cut her off.

"There's something wrong with Melissa. She seems really off today."

"I haven't seen her. The second I came in, she sent me down to the warehouse for a tour of all the product."

"She's grouchy. I mean, more than usual."

Winter considered this. "She seems to be a fairly equal mix of grouchy and friendly."

"Depends on what gender you are." Helen's lips thinned. Then she shook her head as if dismissing herself. "I saw a bruise on her arm. It looks like a handprint."

Winter straightened on her bench. "A handprint?"

"I think Nathan made her stay late last night."

"And you think he…?"

"He can be rough sometimes, especially when he's mad about something."

The tone in Helen's voice made Winter wonder if she was speaking from direct experience. "Helen?"

She dropped her hands in her lap and stared hard at the climbing wall opposite, refusing to make eye contact. "Melissa was the first, I think. At least at Cumberland. She's been dealing with it for so long, she kind of laughs at people who try to lodge complaints. People like Parker. And especially someone like Christina."

"Why do you think that is?"

"Well." She sighed, attempting to hide a slight shiver. "I once tried to ask her about it. She figured she survives just fine, so no one else has reason to complain."

Winter thought back to her experiences with the clearly jaded marketing executive. "I don't know. She doesn't seem like she's 'just fine' with the way Nathan does business."

"That's just 'cause he hasn't asked her to stay late in a long time. Said he was sick of her, allegedly."

Yesterday, when he overheard Melissa flirting with that detective, he'd flown off the handle. If Nathan viewed Melissa as his property, even if he wasn't especially interested in her, he might still want everybody else to keep their hands off.

The man saw himself as a sultan, and this place was his harem.

Yet Mullaney thought he had a solid alibi.

There was no way around it. She needed to move the investigation along. "I need to get closer to Nathan."

Helen gave her a look like she smelled something bad. "I really wouldn't advise that. It's already clear how interested he is in you. I haven't seen him shine up to a new girl like that since…"

"Christina."

Helen's shoulders slumped, and her hands clasped together hard on the tabletop. "Why didn't I warn her? What the hell is wrong with me?"

Helen's sob hit Winter like a stiletto. She closed her eyes and shook her head. "I think you've been traumatized. And Melissa. And Christina too. When that happens, you can't always predict or understand how to act. You do what you have to do to survive."

She sniffled and looked away. "That's a bullshit excuse."

"No, it's not. And it's not your fault. It's not."

Finally, she looked back at Winter. Mascara clung under her eyes, her cheeks flushed and red. "What if Nathan's a murderer?"

"All we have right now is rumors and conjecture. It's nothing. It's not enough." Winter touched Helen's hands lightly. "But I'm going to find out the truth. Hurting you and other women who work for him. Maybe even killing his employees. I'm going to get him to tell me. Or show me his true nature. Even if he hasn't done anything criminal, we can still gain evidence to file a civil suit against him and bring him down."

Slowly, Helen straightened and stood. Then set her jaw hard. "Stay late. That's all you have to do. Stay late, make sure he knows you're staying late, and wait for him to come to you."

Before Winter could figure out what to say, Helen got up, crossed the courtyard, and let the door to the building swing shut behind her.

Winter kept her seat for a moment, just letting the sunshine soak into her skin. She thought of going after Helen, but there was nothing she could say that would make any of this easier.

It wasn't Helen's fault. Trauma did unpredictable things

to people. It could break them, remake them. Twist them with scar tissue.

She took out her phone and texted Noah six words that felt like a betrayal.

I have to stay late tonight.

Then she rose from the table and returned to the sales office, where the air conditioner blew away the afternoon heat.

Winter passed Melissa's computer as she made her way to her desk and sat down. At first, the sound was so quiet that Winter didn't know what she was hearing.

Melissa sat incredibly still, hiding behind her own long blond hair. Quietly sobbing.

21

Though Kline complained when Noah dropped him off at home before heading to Carl Gardner's place of business, Noah could spot a liability when he saw one, and Kline was an untrustworthy dinosaur with a hand injury. He simply didn't want to be worried about protecting anyone else. Some jobs were made for lone wolves, and this was one of them.

Noah had little to go on so far. Gardner's meeting with Ariel, at the very same coffee shop the remote cameras were being routed through, was his strongest piece of evidence. Which was to say, it was circumstantial, leaving a lot of room for doubt.

But Noah had a strong feeling about this one. At last, he had a suspect. But he wanted confirmation before he shared any of this with Winter.

The building at Gardner's address was nondescript, exactly like every other building in this area of town. Gravel sidewalks, wide roads, everything designed to accommodate semitrucks on industrial business. Across the way was a rock company selling flagstones and crushed sandstone for landscaping. Next door, a brewery supply company. Noah parked in that lot next to a big white van, then got out and began to circle the place on foot.

An array of satellite dishes covered the roof. He whipped out his phone, prepared to call the forensic tech down at the office to ask them to tap into the feed, when he paused.

If Eve was hesitating to help him, what chance did he have with anyone else at the office? The odds weren't great. But this case seemed to be about computers and technology, which was hardly his area of expertise. Maybe if he called his tech guy back in Richmond…

Noah was still mulling this over when he turned a corner and nearly bumped into Carl Gardner. The man froze, and his eyes widened with palpable recognition. There was no doubt in Noah's mind this guy knew exactly who he was. And the flash of fear that paled his skin was akin to a confession.

"Hey." As Noah started toward him, Carl flinched and ran into the office building, slamming the door hard behind him. "Oh, no, he didn't." Noah went to the door and pounded with a clenched fist. "FBI! Open up!"

No answer. In the back of his mind, Noah heard a vague cautionary whisper. *Don't do it. If Falkner finds out, he'll eat your ass for breakfast.*

Screw it. Taking out his gun and holding it at compressed ready—held tight to his chest, muzzle level to fire—Noah rounded on the door. Backed by the force of over two hundred pounds, his heavy boot hit the sweet spot, exploding the weak door into a mist of tiny splinters.

He rushed inside, checking his blind spots. The room was empty. But two long tables lined a corner, strewn with monitors. A single high-backed gamer chair was at the center. Empty bags of Fritos and Sour Patch Kids littered the floor, and a wall of empty Mountain Dew cans, meticulously stacked, towered behind the chair. In the far corner was a curved TV screen the size of church doors, a VR rig hooked up to it.

Carl Gardner clearly didn't have much of a life outside of this room. The rank smell of musty BO was proof enough of that.

Then he saw it on one of the monitors. The feed from the camera he'd found, aimed squarely at Winter's office. The focus was on Ariel's desk. She was back at work now, typing away.

Noah ran for the back door, down a short hall and past a bathroom, to an exterior door that led into a disused loading zone. His eyes stung as he stepped back into the sunlight, sweeping his gaze from side to side.

An engine revved, and tires peeled out. Carl Gardner.

The head start he'd gotten was too great. Noah couldn't get to his truck to follow in time. But maybe that wasn't such a bad thing as, in his haste to get away, Carl had just granted Noah full access to everything he'd come here to find.

Grunting at the loss all the same, Noah made his way back to the windowless pit filled with glimmering computer screens. He took a pair of neoprene gloves from his back pocket and slipped them on before tapping on the keyboard. The last thing he needed were his prints all over this place.

He scanned through several different camera angles, using his phone to snap a picture of each one so that, later on, he'd be able to track down all the stray cameras.

There were more than a dozen. Some at the office, and some pointed right at their home. And there were others watching a place that Noah had never seen before—what looked like a big and very expensive house nestled on a large plot of land with trees all around. There were cameras peeking into rooms with vaulted ceilings and honey-colored wooden floors. He'd have to ask Winter if it meant anything to her.

Whoever was watching Winter was monitoring somebody else just as closely. But who?

As he took a step back, the heel of Noah's boot caught a tangle of cables, yanking on one of the monitors. It crashed to the floor, the LED screen splitting into dozens of lines. Noah crouched to study what remained of the image. It looked like a chatroom, the kind where an updating feed constantly scrolled new comments like credits at the end of a movie. He looked closer, trying to decipher anything useful.

Only the lower left corner of the screen was still intact. A new comment populated, and Noah was able to make out just the beginning.

If you think the police can keep Justin caged up, then you're a traitor just like...

Noah's blood turned to ice. This was one of Justin's fan sites. It had to be. And the man who'd been following Winter—sending her creepy texts and unsettling the hell out of them both—was a member.

There'd be no more taking refuge in unconfirmed possibilities. This was happening. The only remaining question was what the hell was he going to do about it.

Noah took a picture of the broken screen. He wished he was more tech savvy so he could really mop up the giant pile of evidence splashed at his feet. As he was thinking about a work-around, he heard the sound of two voices approaching the door from outside.

Stay or go?

The question circled through his head like a spinning top. He'd already overstepped his bounds pretty severely just getting here, but so far, the only person who'd seen him was Gardner. Additional witnesses would only increase the chances of all this getting back to Falkner. Besides, what if those two people were some of Justin's followers? What might happen to Noah's career if he really did have to discharge his weapon while on administrative leave?

Nothing good.

Begrudgingly, Noah turned from the computers and made his way out the back.

22

"Are you okay?" Winter took a cautious step closer to Melissa.

Sniffling, Melissa wiped her eyes with the backs of both hands and retrained her attention on her computer. "I'm fine." She cleared her throat, pushing back squeaks and raspy catches. "Are you ready to learn the customer order forms?"

Winter shrugged and rolled a chair closer to Melissa's desk, then sat down beside her. "It's okay. I promise I won't judge."

"You think I give a damn if you judge me?" Melissa spat, not looking up. Her hand was on the mouse, presumably navigating toward the customer order forms. "Everybody else does. Why should you be any different?"

Winter bit her lip and looked down. This was a delicate situation. It seemed like Melissa wanted to talk about whatever was bothering her. At the same time, she had a tough exterior, the kind of person who would be appalled to develop a reputation for crying at work. If Winter was going to get anything out of her, she had to play her cards very deliberately.

"It seems everybody around here's been out of sorts lately. Helen and I were just talking about everything with the cops and Parker and Aliyah. And she was nearly in tears."

"I don't give a..." Melissa cut herself off, even as her shoulders lifted with tension. "It doesn't matter. I'm fine. I'm always fine. That's what I do."

"Can I tell you a secret?"

Melissa furrowed her brow and finally turned to look at Winter. The expression on her face was heartbreaking. Her eyes like tunnels effectively concealed her secrets, but the red streaks from thick tears on her cheeks told another story.

She wasn't about to open up to some random new girl, but maybe if Melissa knew who Winter really was...

It was risky, but this wasn't the type of situation where Winter could afford to play things entirely safe. People were dying. Everybody in the office was a potential future victim. Sometimes, lies helped keep people safe. Other times, only the truth could do that.

Still, Winter hesitated. If she confided in the wrong person and the truth of who she was got back to Nathan, all this would've been for nothing.

"I'm not actually any good at sales."

Melissa coughed out a dry laugh and shook her head. "Good thing that isn't why Nathan hired you."

"Why did he hire me?" Her voice was soft. Honest.

"You can't be nearly as a naive as you pretend to be." Melissa showed her an incredulous sneer. "I don't buy it."

"If I wasn't naive, would you tell me why you're crying?"

"I'm not crying." She swiped tears away from her eyes.

"Helen said you stayed late last night. With Nathan."

"So what if I did?" she snapped, immediately on the defensive.

"I said I'm not here to judge you, and I mean it." Winter kept her gaze on Melissa's face, hoping to catch her gaze. "I just noticed how angry he got when he caught you flirting with that cute detective yesterday."

"Because Nathan Lynch owns everything. He owns everything, he knows everything, and he's never wrong."

"Charming."

She snorted her agreement. "He's like some kind of fucked-up King Midas. Everything he touches, he turns into his possession. And like a five year old, even if he gets bored with one of his toys and doesn't play with it anymore, he still throws a tantrum if anybody else tries to."

The word *toys* was like a hot poker stamping into Winter's brain. The muscles in her face tightened. "Did he hurt you?"

Melissa let go of the mouse and folded her hands in her lap. "I'm fine."

Winter wanted to say more. Probe her with a dozen questions. Instead, she went quiet. She could tell Melissa really did want to talk about it. Maybe if she just gave her some room.

The flush of a distant toilet broke the silence.

"I had a date last night. He was supposed to meet me here, so I stayed after. I wasn't thinking about Nathan. I figured he'd had his fun making me look pathetic in front of Detective Jallow. I figured that would be the end of it."

Winter chewed on her bottom lip to keep herself from jumping in.

"I heard a voice in the hallway, and I thought it might be my date, so I got up and went out to the atrium. But no one was there. Then Nathan walked in and…one thing led to another."

"You mean you slept with him?"

She smiled—a defensive expression if ever there was. "Yeah. Me and Nathan screw sometimes. So what? He got jealous, felt like he needed to assert himself. What's so wrong with that?"

"You tell me."

She rubbed her shoulder, and Winter wondered if that might be the spot where Helen had seen a bruise on her earlier. Melissa was wearing a cashmere cardigan now. Except her office got a lot of afternoon sun, and it was hot in there.

"Did he force himself on you?"

"No!" Melissa answered too quickly. "Nathan's a lot of things, but he isn't a rapist. I don't care what Christina said. He wouldn't do that. Feeling needed and wanted is what guys like him get off on. He'll coerce, he'll pester, he'll wear you down. But in the end, if you don't say yes, I don't think he'd be able to get it up."

There was so much wrong with that thought process that the only thing Winter felt comfortable with saying was, "Oh."

She turned to Winter with a twisted smile. "You ought to keep that in mind, sweetie. Because he's got a hard-on for you a mile long."

Winter suppressed her shudder. "If you could get Nathan in trouble for the things he does, would you?"

"What do you mean *trouble*?"

"I mean…like Parker. He tried to sue him for sexual harassment, right? Would you ever want to do something like that?"

Melissa shook her head. "Men like Nathan don't go down over a little bit of grab-ass here and there."

"Maybe that was true in the past, but things are different now. Men far more powerful than him have lost everything—"

"I told you, he's not a rapist. And he's smart. He takes videos of himself…I mean…"

"What?"

Melissa tightened her hands in her lap. "Nathan likes to watch. There're cameras in his office. If you go in there with him, you're going to be recorded. He doesn't use the videos for blackmail or put them online or anything. He just holds onto them for his own personal use. Like trophies, I guess." Her mouth curled like she'd just sipped on sour milk. "Anyway, he can also use them to prove all the women he sleeps with said yes."

Winter wanted to slap Melissa upside her head and ask her what the hell was wrong with her, but she was pretty sure she already knew. Clearly, Nathan Lynch wasn't the first man who'd used her in that way. He wasn't the first man to make her feel like her body wasn't her own property. Melissa played along with every comment, every twitch of interest from men. She let them do what they wanted and then tried to lie low.

It was a way to keep herself safe, a defense mechanism learned from years of sexual trauma.

"Do you think Parker had grounds for his case?"

"Yeah, of course he did."

"I mean, clearly, he's an HR nightmare." Winter leaned forward. "But do you know of anything Nathan has done that might be considered criminal?"

"Other than the cameras he put all over the office without anyone's knowledge or consent?"

"Cameras other than is private office?" Winter's heart skittered.

"In other offices, in the break room, running along the floor in the hall, in the bathroom."

"The bathroom?"

"And the locker room and the gym and the changing areas…"

"Why?"

Melissa snorted and flicked her eyes up and down Winter's body. "Three guesses, honey."

A chill racked her body that Winter couldn't repress. She'd used the bathroom in the building.

She didn't want to let herself get distracted. "Has he ever used forceful coercion?"

"Huh?"

"I mean, threatening to fire you if you don't have sex with him?"

"Not me, no. Not out loud anyway. I think that's more of an implied threat. I also think that's the reason Christina left, and Aliyah. Because of the implication."

"Do you have any idea what happened to Aliyah? Where she might be?"

"What are you, writing a book?" Melissa narrowed her eyes, scrutinizing Winter coldly. "Or are you a cop?"

"No. I'm just nervous about everything going on around here. Can you blame me?"

Melissa didn't look convinced. She rose from her desk, snatching her purse as she moved. "I think you're gonna have to find someone else to glom onto for the rest of the day. I'm going home."

"I'm sorry. I didn't mean to upset you."

"It's my stomach that's upset," Melissa snarled, storming out of the office without another word.

23

I never would've imagined such a thing was possible, but Hicks died entirely too quickly. Almost as soon as the body went limp, a sense of horror flashed over me. What had I done? I'd always been so good at planning. Patient, discriminate, even conniving. Never once had I let my feelings and impulses rule me as they had these past weeks.

I blame you, of course. You showed me that I still had a heart in there. And promptly shattered it to pieces.

But Hicks died so fast. I didn't even have a chance to tie him up properly before his heart gave out. I must've been angry, driving the knots down onto his throat.

I wasn't sorry he was dead, just that I wasn't allowed to fully appreciate his suffering while I was so wrapped up in my own thoughts. Worse still, when all was done and that glorious feeling of catharsis swept over me—leaving my body quieted and my skin cooled—I found myself with a dead body to hide. Still during work hours with customers swarming throughout the building, not to mention everyone who worked here.

"You're so stupid and weak." My father would always say

that. *"Just like your mother. You were supposed to get my brain and your mother's looks, but of course, you fucked up and got it backward."*

I saw his sneer as he turned from where I lay, bleeding from my mouth and my ear, thoroughly castigated for the crime of being me.

What would the old man think if he could see me now? Someday soon I'd have the answer to that question.

That day when I told you a little about my father—I was already in love with you by then—your gentle kindness sealed it. You were so much like my mother. I should've known the death sentence inherent in that.

I was unable to move Hicks's body because of Melissa. She stayed late, like she often did, desperate for an opportunity to be used again. And used she was, more roughly than ever before. A hand on her throat, spit on her face, her lean and tight body twisted like a broken marionette.

Sometimes, I wanted Melissa dead more than any of the others. Other times, I was able to appreciate how honestly and completely she succumbed. The woman knew exactly what she was and what she was good for. She didn't pretend to be something else. Not like Aliyah or Helen or any the rest. Melissa wore her shame and depravity like a badge. She took all the punishment meted out to her with whatever grace such a creature like her could muster.

She would be one of the last to die.

All afternoon and evening, Hicks's body sat in a locked custodian's closet. The cleaners came early every morning and would go in there to fetch out vacuums and floor polishers. So after everyone else had finally gone home, I dragged the body out to my ride and tossed it in the back. It was already starting to stink.

Starving and twitchy with anxiety, I drove home and

threw his body into the large chest freezer in my man cave off the garage, displacing blocks of frozen meat and bags of vegetables to make room.

Then I sat there, thinking about where I'd leave him. In the same ravine as Parker and Aliyah, of course. All the bodies left in the same location for better…and for much, much worse.

But the cops would be watching my drop-offs now. Luckily, I knew another way in. It was a longer drive that took me over a bridge to the other side of the forest, and the walk to get to the ravine was longer, but I could handle it. Still, it would take some time and a good amount of energy. Energy I lacked somewhat after the long day I'd had.

And all I could think about was Aliyah and how they hadn't found her body.

Why can't you do anything right? How hard can it be to die at the bottom of a cliff?

If she was somehow still alive, it was my fault. I'd failed to finish her off. But I wasn't about to leave that loose end flapping in the breeze. I was confident she didn't have any information that would help the cops track me down. And there was a good chance she was dead by now, from exposure or starvation.

But what if my confidence was misplaced? What if she recognized my gear? My goggles? The shape of my body or the sound of my voice? What if, against all odds, she was somehow alive?

Unfortunately, I had no choice but to find her and finish her off. But I was drained and emotionally exhausted from Hicks.

I lay down in bed last night thinking about you, wishing you were beside me.

I would've made you my wife. Someday. I don't think I ever told you that.

Still, as I drifted off to sleep, it wasn't your eyes I saw gazing lovingly into mine, but the ice-blue coolness of someone new. Samantha Drewitt, a winter storm. She was on top of me, rocking back and forth so her gorgeous breasts bounced. All natural and pale as moonlight.

As I got hard, I imagined my hands on a rope, drawing knots tight around her body. A noose around her neck, suspended from the ceiling. I watched the fear as it flared in her eyes, as she knew her life was in my hands. When I saw that fear, my body exploded with spasms of delight, filling up her insides.

Would she let me do that to her? I doubted it. She wasn't like the others. *Just like you were not like the others. A purity too beautiful to ever be broken.*

You were as delicate as virgin snow, and they'll all pay for stepping on you.

I woke early this morning and, leaving Tucker exactly as he was, went out to the wilderness preserve to look for Aliyah. There were no police there. Search and Rescue probably already canvassed this location and moved deeper in. But they'd left their yellow tape around my crime scene. I followed a series of flags marking a trail of blood—Aliyah. But those ended at the stream that wound through the very bottom of the ravine.

She was alive. Or at least, she had been. When the sun began to crest over the cliffs, and I heard the first distant barks of a dog out on a morning walk, I knew I couldn't linger any longer. My presence at the dump site would be almost as compelling to a jury as a taped confession. And I couldn't go to prison. I wouldn't. Not to mention, this was Texas. The death penalty was always on the table.

If I were caught, I'd find a way to kill myself quickly. I was not going to be forced to suffer the psychological torture of languishing in a cell for years while I patiently waited for bureaucrats to finish the job.

My workday passed without incident, and at quitting time, I made my way out to the parking lot. I was behind the wheel of my vehicle, my brain churning with thoughts of Aliyah and Tucker and what I could do to make the whole situation right, when I looked up and happened to see two women leaving the building.

Helen Marchand and, at her side, the new girl.

"Samantha." I whispered her name, enjoying the sweet taste of it. "What is Helen saying to you?"

I watched Helen get her keys out, her full lips flapping as Sam listened intently.

"She's probably telling you the same thing she told Christina." I leaned forward on my steering wheel, knowing the glare of the sun on the windshield would hide me. "She's trying to change you. Teach you how to be like Melissa. Giving you lessons. Give in to your baser instincts. Forget who you are. Let men use your body to satisfy their sick desires."

My hands tightened on the wheel, my knuckles turning white. The creak of the leather made me long for the strain of a rope, this one secured tightly around Helen.

"I'd never treat you like that, Samantha. I'd protect your purity. Let you make your own choices. You're better than the other women here, so much better. All you need is a strong hand to guide you."

An image of my mother flashed through my mind's eye. On her knees, tears streaking her beautiful face, her clothes disheveled. *She'd once been like you, but my father was a cruel man.* He debauched her, broke her, bent her to his will. Until the only option to save herself was to end it all and leave me all alone.

"Don't let her hug you, Sam!" *Helen's filthy.*

Samantha and Helen said goodbye. The beautiful one

headed back into the building, while the foul one got into her car and turned the ignition.

I watched Sam until she disappeared inside, the curve of her legs strong and scintillating. I could only imagine how they'd feel under my fingertips—soft and taut all at once.

As Helen pulled out of the lot, I turned over my own engine and followed. I wasn't going to let her do to Sam what she did to my sweet Christina. Helen deserved to be punished. And unlike with Tucker, I was going to take my time.

Tonight, when I returned to the forest, I'd have two bodies with me.

24

Winter knew Cumberland wasn't a real job—just an extension of what she always did. But that fact did nothing to ease the bone-deep exhaustion she felt when five o'clock rolled around and she was finally able to clock out for the day.

She took small detours on the way to her office, berating herself the whole time. Ever since the abrupt and unhelpful end of her conversation with Melissa, Winter had been kicking herself. After all these years, she should've figured out how to be a bit more discreet with her interrogations.

Yet she couldn't stop herself from falling into cop mode. Was Melissa truly suspicious that Winter might be some kind of undercover narc? Or was she just sick of answering questions?

Moreover, there was still no word on Aliyah Andry. If they didn't find her by sundown, she'd be spending her fifth night in the wilderness. If she was lucky enough to be alive.

When Winter arrived at her office, Noah was there waiting. She was hardly surprised. He'd been on edge ever since she'd taken the case, especially with her "parading around" in skimpy outfits to lure the eye of a man who might or might not be a rapist and murderer.

She knew Noah's protectiveness came from a place of love, but that didn't stop her being a bit annoyed. She wasn't a baby, and she didn't need a sitter, not even Noah.

"Hey, stranger." She dropped next to him on the loveseat in her office and gave him a peck on the temple. "What are you doing here?"

"I found the man who's been watching the office."

Her eyebrows lifted as she set her purse down and sank down beside him. "And?"

"It's exactly what we thought. One of Justin's fans. His name is Carl Gardner."

Even as her heart sank, Winter steeled herself. She wasn't surprised or disappointed. All she could feel was a sense of danger, an urge to fly, fight, or freeze. "Okay. I assume there's more to this story…"

"I found another camera and was able to trace the IP. He's got cameras all over the city set up on a router that lets him piggyback on other people's secured Wi-Fi. I had to call in a favor from Eve—"

"I thought you were on leave…"

"One little trace!" He threw his hands in the air. "Why's everybody making such a big deal out of it?"

"Because it is a big deal. You're supposed to be running a tight ship. Not stepping a toe out of line."

"Are you saying you're mad at me for tracking down the SOB who's been making our lives a living hell? Filming you everywhere you go?"

Winter cringed, remembering what Melissa had said about Nathan and the camera in the bathrooms. "It's the twenty-first century. We're all on camera all the time, aren't we?"

"What's that supposed to mean?" He scoffed. "I found his

office. The place with all his computers. I have pictures of the location of all the cameras. And I saw him logged into one of Justin Black's fan sites."

That made her skin crawl. When he was still active, Justin had made a neat little fortune broadcasting his antics on the dark web for a worldwide audience. Winter had never watched any of the videos, at least not any more than was necessary. But she knew she was in some of them. A guest star, a victim…the sideshow freak Justin tried to turn her into.

She closed her eyes and took a deep breath through her nose. "Does he know you've been to his office?"

"I went there just to talk to him, but he ran when he saw me, so I had to kick his door in. Also, I damaged a monitor while I was there."

"Great. So now he has all the time in the world to move his operation and tighten security."

"Whatever." Noah stood and paced to the other side of her office, his hand on the back of his neck. He scratched at his own skin. "You know what, darlin'? I don't give a damn if you're mad at me over this. What kind of husband would I be if I let this go on? Who knows what they might be planning? What if they want to…" His brows tightened, anger flashing in his eyes. "…recreate what Justin did to you? Or even tie up his unfinished business?"

From another man, Winter might've taken such words as nothing more than blustery bullshit. But not from Noah. The rage in her heart didn't soften, but it pivoted away from him and toward the person who truly deserved it. "I'm sorry."

Noah acknowledged her apology with a small nod. "There's one more thing I gotta tell you." He stepped back to the loveseat and got down on a knee in front of her. "I think Ariel might be working with him."

"What?" Winter glanced through the blinds toward Ariel's empty desk and shook her head. "No way."

"I saw her. She met with him. And they seemed to have had a real serious conversation. Like she was giving him details, and he was writing everything down."

"No. I don't...no. I trust Ariel."

"I need you to use your head. Not your heart. People lie. And they do terrible things. Nobody's exempt from that. Not employees, not friends, not family..."

She pressed both her hands over her face and curled her back. "I don't think I can take much more of this."

"I'm sorry." He scratched his neck again. "But in a way, this is all good news. We have a lead now, which means we have a leg up."

"I know." She dropped her hands and looked into his eyes, soaking up one of the only people in the world she could trust. "All this, and everything happening at Cumberland... it's just a lot."

He brushed his heavy fingers lightly over her hair. "What happened?"

"Lynch did it. I can feel it in my bones. And even if he isn't a murderer, he's still a monster. What he's done to the women who work for him..." She moistened her dry lips with the tip of her tongue. Then she reached out and clasped Noah's hand.

An old trick her Gramma Beth taught her from her many years of marriage. Sometimes, when you're irritated with your husband, the best thing you can do is grab his hand and squeeze.

"I heard a rumor that he has cameras in his office so he can record all his late nights with the women there."

"Well, that's not right."

Winter snorted. "That's exactly what I said."

Noah's face darkened as the implications of what she was

saying set in. "I'm not above breaking his back. You say the word."

Winter laughed. It hurt and felt good all at once. "The videos might be exactly what we need to get criminal charges filed against him. Once those come to light, I imagine everything else will too."

"I wish I could be in there with you."

"So do I."

Noah returned to his seat on the couch and threw his arm over her shoulder. She leaned into his chest and breathed in his smell. It grounded her.

"I called Lyle on the way here. The DNA results are in. It was Aliyah Andry's blood on those rocks. But they haven't found her yet."

"Maybe you could take me over to the crime scene. I might see something y'all missed."

"You very well might." The thought of returning to the crime scene generated an unexpected smile on Winter's lips. Going back there meant she'd get to rappel down the wall again. Better yet, she'd get to do it with Noah. "Okay. Let's go."

"Settle down, darlin'. I'm starving. What do you say we get some ribs and talk about all this? Then you can take me over to the site first thing tomorrow morning."

Winter grumbled, her hopes of a late-night rappelling session evaporating, but she didn't argue.

"You win." She stood and walked toward her desk to fetch her phone from her purse. She'd heard it buzz a couple of times.

Her friend, Autumn Trent, had sent her a meme. Gramma Beth had left a voicemail. And someone with an unlisted number had sent her a text that self-deleted before she was able to open it.

"What is it?" Noah stepped up behind her and gazed over her shoulder at the phone in her hand.

"It came in at 1:28…"

He read the time stamp on the message. "That would be right before I turned up at Carl Gardner's office. Hours ago."

Exhausted with all of it, she passed her phone over to Noah to take a look. "If that means something to you, maybe you ought to just hold on to my phone during the day. I have a burner with me while I'm undercover anyway."

"We're gonna catch him." He clicked off the phone and slipped it into his pocket. "We will."

Winter sighed. As they passed Ariel's desk on their way out, her mood darkened. "You ought to know better than to make promises, Agent Dalton."

25

Helen pulled into her driveway, her clammy hands trembling on the wheel. The whole ride home she'd been trying to strong-arm her own brain into thinking about anything other than the situation.

Music didn't help. Neither did her favorite comedy podcast. She even tried calling her mother to distract herself, but she'd been on her way to a singles salsa-dancing class. Then, in a last-ditch effort, she went to her favorite natural grocery store to stock up on healthy food for the weekend. Healthy body, healthy mind.

Yeah, right, like a crown of broccoli's going to magically erase my worries.

At least Helen felt grateful to be home, away from prying eyes and wandering hands. When she blinked, the tears she'd been holding back all day descended. Her mind was turning over what might happen if or when Winter stayed late to be with Nathan. Helen had clear memories of the first time she'd done that exact thing, memories that she'd tried to repress for years. Sometimes with alcohol, sometimes just with rationalizations.

The worst thing about it wasn't that he'd forced himself on her. He hadn't. He'd been smooth, charming, and good-looking, everything a woman could ever ask of a man. And even though Melissa had warned her Nathan was a womanizing bastard, she hadn't really listened. Not when she was brand-new to the company. Nathan had showered her with attention, and she had soaked it all up, believing he might actually think she was special.

God, she was so stupid back then. She gave herself to him, let him do what he wanted. And though she'd never once admitted the truth to another soul, never even said it out loud, it wasn't because she was afraid of him or thought she might lose her job. She'd genuinely thought he liked her, and she had liked him. Honestly, she'd found the idea of an affair with the boss kind of sexy.

And it had been, until it wasn't. When she saw who Nathan really was and how he operated—the way he treated every single woman in the office—Helen was disgusted. And she had wanted nothing more than to pull away from him and tell him what a creep he was. But by then, it was too late.

She'd gotten used to the salary and the benefits, used to everything Cumberland had to offer. So although she died a little inside every time, she let Nathan keep touching her. Kept playing the role of the submissive little work mouse until she couldn't take it anymore. But he'd broken her heart long before that.

The investigator would never let anything like that happen to her. She was so much smarter and stronger than Helen was. In fact, there was a time when Helen had thought everybody in the world was stronger and smarter. Sure, Melissa and the others were coerced into bed with Nathan, too, but they'd never been stupid enough to actually develop feelings for the monster.

That was the real reason Helen never said a word to

Christina, or Aliyah, or any of the new hires who came through Cumberland's doors. She kept her shame to herself, confident that anybody could handle the situation better than she had.

Two days after Christina died, Nathan asked Helen to come to his office just as she was about to head home. He seemed distraught, as if he really gave a damn about what had happened to their colleague. They talked about it a little, Nathan showing her that poetic and gentle side of himself that had first drawn her to him years ago. Helen wasn't sure if it was a lie. In fact, she was certain there was an aching, bleeding heart under all his callous crustiness.

Then he started touching her.

Disgusted, Helen pulled away. For the first time ever, she said no. The flash of anger in his eyes was the most terrifying thing she'd ever seen. In a moment, everything about him changed. His face was dead as he grabbed a fistful of her hair and yanked her close.

Helen was too shocked to struggle. His other hand encircled her throat, and he pushed her to her knees. He choked her and forced her to open her mouth, all the while telling her how much she liked it.

When it was done, he kissed her on the mouth, told her she was a good girl, and threw her out of his office with all the care of a used tissue.

After she staggered home that night, Helen leaned over her bathroom sink looking at her own bloodshot eyes and swollen lips. Then and there she decided that she wasn't going to let him get away with it ever again.

She found Winter Black—one of the only woman private investigators in Austin. Helen couldn't bear the thought of telling her story to a man. So far, she hadn't even gotten up the courage to tell Winter all the facts, though she fought to every time they spoke.

Helen balled a fist and punched the wheel, then slipped out of her car and started for her front door—the house she was only able to afford because of Cumberland and Nathan Lynch's generous bonuses. She was going to stop him. Winter was going to stop him. And then maybe Helen's nightmares would stop too.

Crap, she'd forgotten the groceries.

Too late, she saw the shadow loom up behind her. She whirled, a scream in her throat, but not before pain exploded all through her skull. Her knees hit the ground hard as she fell, and before she could get back up, something wrapped tightly around her throat.

Her hands clawed wildly at black leather gloves and rope, but all the energy drained from her in what felt like seconds. Like sinking into dark water. Her last thought before she succumbed to the blackness was that Nathan had found out about Winter—found out what Helen was trying to do. And now, he was going to punish her for it.

❄

Helen came to, goaded to consciousness by a painful bump on her head. But waking provided no relief from her nightmare.

As starlight filtered in through foggy black windows, she realized she was lying in the cargo area of some vehicle. She tried to touch the throbbing wound on her head, but her hands wouldn't move.

All at once, she realized she was tied up. Green rope, showing vaguely gray in the dim light, was wrapped around her hands and her ankles, knots climbing up her thighs and over her chest. Her throat was tight, a rope threaded over and over against her skin. And her tongue was gagged by a rope ball, the rough texture scratching the sides of her mouth. More lengths of rope wound tight around the back of her head.

Her first hunch had to be right. This was Nathan, punishing her. The ropes burned against her flesh. Helen blinked tears from her eyes and struggled against the knots, the memory of Nathan's hand around her throat tearing through her nerves. Choking her, controlling her breath. Controlling every part of her.

The hatchback opened, and a man stared down at her. Dressed in black with a mask and goggles and gloved hands. A coil of rope was thrown over one of his shoulders. He was tall, lean, and muscular with all the humanity of a robot. He could've been Nathan. He looked like every mountain-climbing prick she'd ever met in that disguise.

He reached for her, and Helen thrashed, screaming from behind the knotted rope. Barely a sound came out. But he didn't grab her. Instead, he snatched up a rope tied to her feet and yanked hard.

Helen fell from the back of the SUV onto gravel with a painful thud.

Then he began to walk, dragging her behind him with grunts of effort. Tiny sharp rocks bit at her skin, getting lodged under the ropes that covered her body like a net. She cried silent tears.

I'm sorry! I never should've hired her!

But she couldn't speak. And the ropes were growing so tight, she couldn't even move.

"You're nothing special, Helen," the man said, his voice deep and gravelly.

Why was Nathan talking like a freak?

So she wouldn't be able to identify him...

Maybe he wasn't planning to kill her. Maybe he just wanted to put the fear of God into her.

Or maybe he was just scared somebody else might see him.

"You know that, though. Don't you? You know you're not as smart as Melissa, as pretty as Aliyah, as pure as Christina. You're nothing, and nobody's going to miss you."

He dropped her in the gravel. She could barely move her head to take in where they were. It was so dark. The smell of trees and dirt filled her nostrils, the taste of blood flooding her tongue.

He picked up the rope tied to her feet again, letting out slack as he went. Helen flopped over to watch as he climbed up the trunk of a tree and tossed the rope over a high limb.

He hopped down. "Thread it through and lock the carabiner." He turned to face her.

In the darkness, all she could see was the glint off his green goggles.

"Wouldn't want any bears getting to you."

Helen's eyes widened as the rope twisted and creaked. Pulling through the carabiner high in the tree, he dragged her closer and closer 'til she was lifted from the ground, hanging by her feet.

She struggled and thrashed, but that only made it worse. The tug of the suspension line only tightened the ropes further, choking off blood to her limbs.

"You won't get away this time."

The man in black wrapped the rope round and round the tree trunk, then tied it tight. He stepped back and set hands on his hips, surveying his work.

As she swayed and reeled, Helen realized another person was hanging from a branch on the other side of the tree. He wasn't wrapped up in knots like she was, merely hanging from a rope lashed to his ankles, his arms dangling limp under him.

Gusty wind blew them, making their bodies spin.

Is he alive? Please, God. Who is he?

It was too dark, and she couldn't get a good look at his face.

"You're wondering about your companion, I see. Just another very un-special person. It's a wonder you two didn't fall in love." He laughed at his own joke and shook out his broad shoulders. "Well, you can be together now. Hang out for a while and think about what you've done…" His voice tightened as if speaking through clenched teeth. "What you *didn't* do, Helen."

The ropes were stopping her blood flow and stealing her air. The pull on her feet seemed to be attached to the knot on her throat, drawing it tighter and tighter with every slight movement. The body hanging a few feet away twisted on its rope, and for a faint second, the starlight caught his face.

Tucker. His ghostly blue skin looked frozen. His empty, sightless eyes stared into nothing.

Dead. He was dead.

Again, Helen screamed against the knotted rope in her mouth. She struggled. The ropes grew tighter and tighter until her vision darkened, blotting out the twinkling night sky.

26

Winter's shift at Cumberland started a little later that morning—it was Saturday—meaning she'd have plenty of time to take her husband into the forest to look at the crime scene.

But the morning brought its own difficulties. Because, despite searching the whole house and calling his phone twice, she couldn't find Kline anywhere. He hadn't said a word to Noah. Winter even called Ariel to ask if she knew anything. It was like he'd just disappeared into thin air.

As Noah packed up the truck for their little excursion, Winter stood in the kitchen sipping her coffee and trying not to care while she scrolled through notifications and text messages on her regular phone. Opal Drewitt had called again. Twice.

Kline.

What if, after Noah's ill-advised raid, this Carl Gardner person decided it was time to be more hands-on? What if he'd taken Kline and was planning on using him to hurt Winter?

Or what if Kline was fine and had left without saying goodbye for no good reason?

She pressed Opal Drewitt's number. Maybe she knew.

It rang before going to voicemail. Winter gave a defeated sigh and hung up. A few moments later, her phone rang. She cleared her throat and answered, "Opal?"

"Hello! I'm sorry I missed your call. I was elbow deep in dishwater."

"No worries. I was just wondering, have you heard from Kline lately?

"Oh, yes. He called me last night and said he was headed back my way for a visit. Did he not mention it to you?"

"Nope."

"That's so like him." Opal scoffed. "Back in the day, I often got close to wringing his neck over that exact same malarkey."

"Men."

"Tell me about it." The sound of clinking silverware and dishes came over the line. "I hope you're doing well. Sorry if I've been driving you crazy with the calls. Nothing urgent. Just thought it'd be nice to have another chat if you're available."

Unexpectedly, Winter brightened at the thought. "Yeah, I'm sorry I keep missing you. Work is crazy and—"

"You don't have to justify yourself to me."

"Thank you," Winter said, and she meant it. "Maybe I can give you a call when I have a bit more time."

"I look forward to that."

They said their goodbyes and hung up just as Noah appeared in the doorway, silently signaling he was ready to go.

She felt confident now that the person on the phone was actually Kline's sister, and for the first time, Winter wondered if she might have just gained a new family member.

※

Noah parked as close to the trailhead as he could. Shouldering a bag of climbing supplies Winter had scored from Cumberland, he followed her through the trees toward the spot where they'd have to gear up with harnesses and descend into the gorge.

She walked in front of him down the narrow trail. Noah kept his eyes mostly on her backside as they went. "So what have you learned about this Aliyah Andry?"

Winter pulled back the limbs of a sapling to pass through, then held it for him. "I know she was the one who helped get Christina her job at Cumberland. I tried to talk to Melissa about it, but she didn't have much to say other than Aliyah was *fine*." She shrugged and turned back to the trail. "Everyone around there is tight-lipped."

"Can't imagine why."

They stepped up to the ledge—a deep ravine with sheer cliff faces going down through twists of knotted trees. Winter grabbed the bag from his shoulder, dropped it on the ground, then leaned down and started pulling out gear. "She's a seasoned climber, verified by everyone at Cumberland."

"If she's spent any real time in the wilderness, she's staying put until she's found." Noah couldn't help but point out the positives.

"Except SAR's already covered ten square miles out from her last known location, and they haven't found her. And there's a killer on the loose."

"Yeah, that'll keep a person moving."

"But she's injured." Winter looked out at the vast forestry.

Noah joined her. The woodland splayed out in all directions, the sun bright in the sky above it. Hard to imagine this majestic location had become a drop zone for a killer. "They'll search up to fourteen days, darlin', and it sounds like Aliyah Andry is a smart young woman, a survivor." Noah gave her his most hopeful smile.

She seemed to relax a little. "Okay," she said, "I have something I want to tell you, but first you have to promise not to go all white knight on me, okay?"

"Excuse me?" He chuckled. But, already, Noah was on edge. His wife was being filmed at her office, stalked while she was undercover. Dressing in skimpy outfits to try to attract attention from a man they were almost positive was a rapist and possibly a murderer.

The urge to go all white knight had rarely been stronger.

Still, he wasn't twenty-five anymore. He knew better than to try to rush in and solve all her problems. Theoretically.

"Tell me."

"Promise."

"Fine, fine. I promise."

Winter pulled out a harness and stepped into it, tightening the hard line around her waist. "You know how I said Lynch has cameras in his office?"

"Uh-huh."

"Well, Melissa thinks he's installed cameras all over the building. Like in the bathrooms and the women's locker room…"

Fire flared like ignited grease in Noah's blood. "You mean he's been filming you…?"

"Down, boy." She set her hand lightly on his chest. "If I can find them, that could be the beginning of the end of all this."

"You will find them. There's no doubt in my mind. But when you do, you're gonna have to tread carefully. We still don't know exactly what this sick SOB is capable of. After the life I've lived, I usually go ahead and assume that anybody is capable of anything."

"Preach." She grabbed the second harness and held it out to him. "You ready for this?"

"Pfft." He took the harness and stepped into it. "This ain't my first rodeo."

Winter cocked one sculpted black eyebrow. "You say that about everything."

"'Cause I've done everything sixteen times at least. I'll be happy to give you some pointers, noob."

She rolled her eyes. "The Marines were a long time ago, old man."

Noah bared his teeth playfully. "You got some dirty laundry?"

"What?"

"I got a washboard you can use." He lifted the bottom of his shirt.

"Glamour muscles." Giggling, Winter slapped his stomach dismissively.

"How dare you."

"You're a Ken doll. Those abs are nice to look at, but I'm not sure you know how to use any of them anymore."

"You wanna fight, Barbie?"

"I know how often you skip leg day."

Noah snatched up the rope. "Lemme go down first, baby girl. That way, I can catch you when you swoon."

"You don't have the grip strength."

"Come over here and lemme give you a squeeze." He opened his arms wide and lunged at her.

"Get away from me!" She ducked out of the way and punched him in the arm. It hurt like it always did. She was so much stronger than she looked.

It was good to be reminded of that from time to time, especially with how worried he'd been about her lately.

They tied into the belay rope, Noah giving Winter unsolicited pointers on her figure-eight knot. Together, they sat back over the ledge. It'd been years since Noah went rappelling, but like riding a bike, his hands and feet knew what to do. His stomach went squirrely, the way it did when he found himself in any potentially dangerous position.

But Noah had learned long ago the trick to transforming nervousness into excitement. Anything that made his body go on edge was a signal that he ought to pay attention to what was about to happen. Thrills often followed.

"You ready, leatherhead?" Winter smiled, the sun glinting off her bright eyes. It was common for the sight of his wife to strike him off-balance, making it hard to think of anything but her.

She dangled from the wall, loose and confident, the verdant green forest all around. He hadn't seen such a free, open, unguarded smile on her face in a long time. Not since that first haunting text came in.

Noah watched as Winter took off down the exposed face, reeling down the cliff and dancing through the air like a crouching tiger.

"Cheater!" He pushed off hard with his feet, sailing down the wall after her. When his hand caught the line again, it was a bit too tight, jerking him. It didn't take long for him to get the hang of the movement again, but long enough he lost an opportunity to gain on Winter.

"Slowpoke!"

He moved as fast as he could, but his eyes were on her. Every time she pushed off from the wall, his heart leaped into his throat, forcing him to regain focus before making his next move.

She touched down first. When her boots hit the ground,

his head cleared, and he made his final approach at lightning speed.

Winter was a little out of breath, still smiling but with a gentle relief in her eyes.

Noah unhooked his carabiner and walked up to her. She met his eyes and settled into a smug grin, ever so pleased about her victory. He wrapped his arm around her waist, pulled her close, and kissed her grinning mouth.

She threw her arms over his shoulders, lifting to her tiptoes as he pulled her body tight against his. His fingers wandered to her butt and squeezed.

Winter squeaked, her arms tightening around his back. "What are you doing? This is a crime scene."

"It's a crime you're so sexy." Noah gave a grunt of acquiescence, then kissed her once more for good measure. Still holding her close, he pressed his forehead to hers. "We should go climbing more often."

"I completely agree." She grinned and kissed the tip of his nose, then pulled away. She took a few steps from the cliff toward a small pile of boulders and pointed. "This is where they found Parker Roy. Just through there is where I found the ropes that were used on Aliyah Andry."

"No way this guy's carrying the bodies down here on his back." Noah craned his neck to see the crest of the cliff high above.

"Oh, he tossed them over the edge, all right."

"It's not so high that a person couldn't survive it."

"They'd be in a hell of a state, though. See that branch?"

"The Ashe Juniper?" Noah studied it. "Yup, looks like it caught your girl. She almost took it down. But then she would've rolled down the cliffside and hit one of these guys." He pointed to the cluster of old cypress trees.

"That's what has me thinking Aliyah has to still be in this area." Winter nodded in agreement. "Deputy Ranger

Babyface said they lost her trail at a stream about half a mile west of here. Farther toward the center, I guess?" She crouched among the rocks, her eyes wide as she searched for details.

Noah knew from experience that both of them tended to see more if they split up. After all, staring at his wife's butt was hardly conducive to uncovering overlooked evidence.

"I'll be back." He readjusted the straps on his backpack, then started away from the wall toward the center of the ravine, where he imagined the stream must be. Aliyah Andry almost certainly knew the killer might be trying to hunt her down. If she was smart enough to head for water to try to mask her scent, she might've been smart enough to find a really good hiding place and stay there.

Noah could only imagine what she had to be going through. If she didn't get to help, she would die from exposure. But if the killer found her…

He heard the giggle of moving water as he emerged from the trees into a small clearing. Every step was hard fought, the brush at his feet thick and prickly even through his thick jeans. He wondered how Aliyah might've been dressed, but Winter had mentioned professional attire, so her outfit couldn't have been ideal for hiking, running, hiding, surviving.

And heels in the forest? Hard to think of worse shoes, but trying to walk barefoot would shred her soles, he had no doubt. Not great options.

When he reached the stream—warm brown water, narrow enough to jump over—Noah crouched and set his fingertips in the silt. The bed was soft mud, not craggy or slippery like some. It would've been easy for even an injured person to keep their balance while walking down it.

Maybe Aliyah was trying to follow the water. Downstream would eventually lead her to a larger river and back to civilization. Based on Aliyah's former job at a mountaineering company, Noah had a feeling Aliyah might know that.

Drawing himself back up, Noah had started to turn in that direction when something above caught his eye. On the far opposite edge of the canyon, a tree grew diagonally up from the cliff face—thick and strong, even with its precarious positioning. One limb stretched far out over the ravine. Dangling from it was an object wrapped in green rope. It almost looked like a giant butterfly cocoon.

Noah moved to get a better angle and saw another object, long and not bound with rope, hanging from another thick branch of that same tree.

He swung his backpack around front and dug into it to take out his binoculars. When he trained them on the tree, he sucked in a cold breath. It was two people, one lashed in ropes and the other dangling by their feet. He zoomed in on the face of the upside-down one as the body twisted in the light wind.

Skin as white as paper. Blue lips and blue veins. Eyes open and empty, drained of life.

27

Back at Cumberland, Winter exited Noah's truck, knowing what she was walking into—an entire building under FBI scrutiny. Members of Austin's Violent Crime Unit were there assisting the rangers, and she imagined Noah's partner Eve would be among them.

Helen was dead, so Winter had no client anymore. Therefore, if she wanted to be cold and clinical about it, she had no reason to continue to involve herself in the investigation. But she couldn't pull out now. For Helen's sake, for Parker, for Aliyah, and for Tucker Hicks too. And for Christina, however she fit into all this. Not to mention for everybody else who was still in danger.

Winter could still make use of the undercover story she'd built. The park rangers could use her. The FBI. What she'd done could blow the case open. Quitting simply because she wasn't being paid anymore never really crossed her mind, apart from a passing observation that she kind of sucked at making money.

When Noah had found the bodies about four hours ago,

he'd called it in. Then they rushed over to secure the scene and direct civilians away from it.

The tree where the bodies were hung was directly across the narrow ravine from the ledge over which the killer had dumped Parker Roy and Aliyah Andry. Naturally, they were still waiting for the official report, but it seemed Helen had been tied up in the same strange and elaborate harness as the first two victims had been, and she died on scene.

Tucker Hicks, on the other hand, had simply been strangled with a rope and strung up by his ankles. There was some indication that his body had been frozen, which made sense to Winter, since he wasn't at work yesterday. He must have been killed on Thursday at some point.

The rangers had called the FBI to assist, and Noah's partner Eve had arrived on scene shortly thereafter. But she'd only relayed that much about the investigation after Winter confessed her undercover story. It was a simple recognition of how much they could help each other. And certainly not an invitation for Noah to help with the case. In fact, Eve kind of refused to look him in the eye.

Winter entered the building and caught Eve's attention. She trusted her husband's partner not to blow her cover. No doubt, Winter would be called to give her own side of the story at some point, but at this very moment, she was Samantha Drewitt.

She was heading down the hall toward Melissa's office when a man's voice called out to her.

"Sam? Can I borrow you for a minute?"

Winter stopped in her tracks. Nathan Lynch.

Once again, she was dressed in a skimpy outfit. Meanwhile Helen, who'd hired her, was in the back of an ambulance being transported to the M.E.'s office for autopsy.

Swallowing her discomfort, Winter turned. She widened

her eyes to feign innocence. She was getting the impression Lynch liked that. "Nathan, hi, sure thing."

"Come into my office for a minute."

Winter nodded and walked through the door he held open for her. After he closed it, he headed back toward his desk.

"Did you hear the latest?" He undid a button on his sports coat as he sat down. Then he gestured for her to take a seat.

She sat down in the chair across from him and pressed her knees together but carefully avoided eye contact, only occasionally glancing up. "Helen. And Tucker. I can't believe it." She was thankful she'd had several hours to process the tragic news before dealing with this guy.

Lynch nodded and looked out the window, squinting in the sunlight. "The police interviewed me first, of course. I don't know why they have it in their heads that I'm some kind of bad guy."

I can't imagine. Winter shook her head and chewed on her lips. "Are you going to be okay?"

"Don't worry about me. I have a solid alibi. I was at home with my family and I had a conference call with some old colleagues. Though there is something very unnerving, and insulting, about having to account for one's whereabouts."

"You're married?"

"Happily." He grinned.

Her stomach turned. "Do you have kids?"

"Two that I'm aware of." His shit-eating grin widened. "Just kidding."

No, you're not.

"Where were *you* last night, Sam? I can't help but notice how all these deaths seem to coincide with when you first came to work for the company…"

Winter's jaw tightened. This was all just a big joke to him. Two people he knew well had just been found tortured and murdered that morning, and he thought there was something funny about that.

A killer gloating over having gotten away with it?

Winter decided to hold tight to her ingenue act. "Last night, I was just at home. I don't…"

"Were you alone?"

"Oh, um—"

"Okay, what I really want to know is, who was that burly guy in the truck? Your boyfriend?"

Winter hooked her foot around the leg of her chair, pressing hard to keep from reaching across the desk to punch him. "My brother. He wanted to take me out to lunch to celebrate the new job."

"Well, isn't that sweet?" His smile grew pensive, his eyes gazing through her. "It's important to keep up family connections. Never forget how lucky you are to have a sibling. Somebody who *knew you when*, as they say."

"Yeah. My brother's great, but he can be a bit overprotective. Do you have any siblings?"

"No. I'm an only child. And I lost my mother some years ago."

She tilted her head in a show of sympathy. "I'm sorry. Were you two close?"

"Yes." His voice remained as dark and smooth as late-night radio, but there was a twitch under one eye. "I loved her. More than anything. I guess you could say I've always gotten along better with women."

Like how a spider gets along with flies.

"I could see that. What about your dad?"

"Yeah, we're the opposite of close." He rose from his seat, dipped a hand into the bin of ropes beside his desk, scooped one up, and started fidgeting. That question had clearly agitated him. "But in all seriousness, I wanted to make sure you're still feeling all right about your new position. I'd be very unhappy if you were scared off by all this police business."

She shrugged, trying to look like she was putting on a brave face. "It *is* scary. I've never known someone who was murdered before."

"I have."

"You mean Parker?"

"No, before then." Lynch sat on the edge of his desk, tying a double fisherman's knot, undoing it, redoing it. Making Winter's skin crawl.

"Really? Who?"

"I'd rather not talk about that." He cleared his throat, dropped the rope, then set both his hands against the edge of the desk and leaned back. His knee brushed hers. "I'd much rather talk about you."

"Me?" She forced herself not to shudder. He was slimier than a bag of carrots left at the back of the fridge. "What about me?"

"I don't think I got a chance to tell you how impressed I was by what you almost accomplished this week."

"You mean the climbing?"

He nodded, his gaze freely wandering over her body now. "It was a real pleasure to watch you. It's not often you meet a woman who's so ready to go after what she wants."

He took her by the hand and guided her to stand. With the seat of the chair pressing against her legs, she couldn't help her chest brushing his. He glanced at her breasts, then back to her eyes.

"I can't stop thinking about your body on that wall."

"Really?" She slipped out around the side of him, freeing herself from the trap set up between the chair and his desk. But he didn't let go of her hand and instead pivoted with her like it was some kind of a dance.

He took a step forward, and she a step back.

"The way you move is incredible. I bet you're pretty flexible."

Her fingers itched to hit him. "Yeah, I am." Winter took another step back.

Nathan pursued in rhythm. "So am I. I'm strong too. I think you saw how easy it is for me to pick you up and put you against the wall."

The look in his eyes said he was going to kiss her. He set his hand on the wall over her shoulder and began to lean in. "Be a good girl, now…"

A thrill of panic brought a flush to her cheeks. Every instinct in her lower half said to drive her patella right into his testicles.

But she couldn't do that.

Winter's skin tightened, and leftover screams from hollow memories of her brother echoed in her ears.

Unwelcome touch, silky and filthy.

Crude oil running over her skin to make everything foul and useless.

Her fists clenched on their own. She'd kill him before she let him kiss her.

Winter rolled out from under his arm and rushed toward the door. "I need to go to the bathroom."

Before he could say a word, she was gone.

She ran down the hall to the nearest exit and burst outside. Cool air rushed over her, breaking the spell that her trauma had cast. But she didn't stop. She kept going, power walking down the path toward the parking lot.

"Get ahold of yourself." She managed a long breath through her nostrils, a calming exhalation from the mouth. Again, and again. She kept walking. She had no car, since Noah had dropped her off. So she continued down the sidewalk toward the string of offices that occupied a strip mall next door, where dozens of people would be working.

Their presence would help keep her safe, at least from someone like Nathan Lynch.

Pacing back and forth in front of a restaurant supply store, Winter took out her phone and called one of the only men alive she actually trusted.

It rang. And rang.

"You have reached Noah Dalton. Please leave your name and number after the tone."

Beep!

"Noah…um…" She swallowed hard, the words catching in her throat. She wanted to tell him everything that had just happened and what she was feeling. But it wouldn't come out. Years and even decades of pretending she was always fine choked out her insides, forcing the feelings down even as they screamed to be let out.

At last, she managed to say something.

"I don't know how much longer I can do this…"

28

Noah sat in Gramma Beth's car—which he'd borrowed especially for the purpose—outside the warehouse where Carl Gardner had his offices. If Gardner were smart, he would've jumped ship by now. But something in the back of Noah's brain told him that wasn't the case. The guy had been rather bold so far, almost like he wanted to be caught.

The hanging tree from that morning still flashed through Noah's brain like strobe lights. Of course, he'd seen a lot of horrible things in his life. Things he carried with him everywhere he went, even if they usually sat silent in the background like the tableau of a nightmare.

But the way Helen Marchand had been wrapped up in nylon rope like something out of a Japanese kink porno... that had Noah worried over this killer's motivation. Clearly, it was all about Cumberland.

Something that happened there...or didn't happen there.

Winter was still convinced Nathan Lynch was the one behind it all, in spite of his *just home with the fam* alibis.

Families lied for each other all the time. It was one of

those things that could be counted on. Like a slice of toast always landing butter-side down when dropped on the floor.

Still, Noah wondered if maybe Winter had pulled a Winter and gotten herself too emotionally involved in the case. Naturally, she'd be convinced Nathan was behind the murders. Dealing with that undoubtably horrible human being, day after day, would lead her to that conclusion.

But being horrible didn't necessarily make a person a murderer. Most horrible people weren't even proper criminals.

The side door of Carl Gardner's office slammed open, and the man himself came strolling out, a can of Mountain Dew in his grasp. Though his quarry was somewhat hidden in the shade of the adjacent building, with his binoculars, Noah could discern dark, baggy circles under bloodshot eyes.

"Nerves getting to you, huh, Carl? Not enough to tuck tail and run." Noah took a sip from his water bottle, feeling smug.

Take that, Weston Falkner.

He watched in silence as Gardner got into his car and drove away. Deciding to join him, Noah rolled onto the empty street. The windows in Gramma Beth's car were all down, inviting in the tepid midday air, and "Holy Diver" blasted from the stereo.

Noah had come prepared this time with every information-getting mechanical gadget he had at his disposal. A rather poor collection compared to what he could've gotten at the FBI, but Eve was on tenterhooks with him. Asking for another under-the-table favor might send her over the edge. He knew why, though. If he got himself canned, she'd be all alone in that windowless office once again. And the plastic bamboo duo weren't the best conversationalists.

He dismissed the possibility of the end of his career with a cold chuckle, reminding himself that he was being ridiculous. Falkner just needed some time to calm down, remind Noah and everybody else of his big-dick energy.

Noah needed to focus on the task at hand.

Slipping out of the car, Noah took the long way around to the back door of the office park. He would've simply used the same door he'd come in through yesterday, but a few two-by-fours had been nailed over it. No doubt, they were going to have to replace the door itself.

When he reached the back door—locked, of course—Noah first put on his gloves then went into his bag and took out his lock picking kit. It wasn't a skill he used too often. The FBI tended to simply break doors down that refused to open. But, as everybody kept reminding him, he was not here representing the FBI. Just another garden-variety delinquent.

The door had a simple warded catch with no dead bolt. Noah was through it in seconds, the lock itself no worse for wear. Nobody would ever know.

He stepped into the hall, quickly orienting himself to the layout. Thin gray carpet muffled the sound of his steps. He wasn't sure if there might be anybody else inside, but it was best to assume there was until he knew better.

When he reached the door to Gardner's office, he paused. It was hanging wide open, just like last time.

Noah drew his weapon and stepped cautiously through, ready to bolt if he smelled a threat.

Once again, the office was empty, save Gardner's incredible mess, which had only increased since yesterday. The monitor Noah had broken had not been moved, but a new one had been installed in its place.

Holstering his gun, Noah leaned down to peer at the screen.

Justin's Right Hand was displayed across the top of the

bare-bones site. Settling a gloved hand on the mouse, Noah clicked the site address and took a picture. A stream of numbers followed by a dot onion domain. Then, he settled into the task of finding out just what the hell was going on in this particular dark corner of the internet.

The site was currently open to a chat room where a scrolling list of comments and usernames continually repopulated the screen. A few people were actively speculating about where Justin was being held. The primary contender was ADX Florence in Colorado. They were sharing blueprints of the place, discussing security detail.

Luckily, their speculation was wrong. Very few people were even aware the prison where Justin was held—ADX Valdez in New Mexico—even existed. But that didn't stop a chill running down Noah's spine.

He hit the back button and was directed to a list of potential chat rooms. As he scrolled the topics, the taste of watery bile filled his throat. It read like a list of Justin's victims, some who lived, some who didn't. One topic heading, *Free the Protégé*, made him wrinkle his nose in confusion, until he clicked it open and read a few lines of conversation.

The chat was all about Timothy Stewart—the little boy who'd been kidnapped by Justin after his entire family was killed in front of him. Winter had been Justin's prisoner at the time. Drugged and tortured, psychologically and physically.

When Winter managed to get away from Justin, he also managed to get away from the police, with little Timothy Stewart as his new captive. The boy spent months under Justin's thumb, enduring untold torture. When eventually Justin was apprehended, Timothy's mind was so warped that he actually fought to try to protect him. He tried to kill

Winter for what she'd done to Justin, and in trying to protect her, Noah took an eight-inch blade in the guts.

He still carried the scar, but that little boy haunted his wife's dreams. When she was thinking about Timothy, a particular distance shadowed her eyes. She had once told Noah that, in a way, she felt closer to Timothy Stewart than anybody else she'd ever known.

That little boy, now older, might be the only person alive who truly understood what Justin put her through.

Anger pulsing like a boil in his brain, Noah clicked back to scan the list of chat rooms. Winter's name wasn't there, but he did find one room that chilled the blood in his veins. It was labeled *Sexy Sissy*.

He was about to click the link when Winter's phone in his pocket chirped with a text message. Noah took a step back from the computer and pulled out the phone to check it.

The message came from a restricted number. *I'm still here, watching you.*

Something in the room beeped, and a notification flashed on one of the other monitors. The same message Noah had just read on Winter's phone was there on the screen, with a one-minute timer ticking off seconds under it.

Literally racing against the clock, Noah did a quick search of the room. He checked under the desks, along the walls, in the corners, inside the air shaft. Nothing.

The text message timer disappeared at the exact moment as the text self-deleted from Winter's phone. Then a new timer popped up, this one counting down from twenty-eight minutes.

There were four computers running the six monitors. Noah traced the cable from the monitor displaying the fan site to the standing processor, then slipped a USB drive inside. It was loaded with software to help it bypass encryptions and automatically copy all files to itself while remaining undetected.

The process took about two and a half minutes, depending on the size of the files.

There was a part of Noah that just wanted to destroy everything in the room. Perhaps he would've, if he'd thought Carl Gardner was a lone wolf. But Noah hadn't gotten that impression. In fact, the more he stared at the disturbingly in-depth and expansive website, the more he suspected Gardner was just one little cog in a much bigger machine.

As Noah browsed the chat, one user—the admin—stood out. While users would banter back and forth, asking and answering questions for one another, sometimes a more authoritative voice chimed in. Username *justinsri8hand*. The admin seemed to have an almost encyclopedic knowledge of Justin's many crimes, not unlike Noah himself.

As he skimmed a shockingly accurate narration from justinsri8hand about the day he was finally arrested, Noah realized there was no way this person could have acquired so much information simply from digging online. Whoever the right hand was, there was no doubt in Noah's mind they'd met Justin. At least once.

The USB program finished running with a pulse of a tiny green light. Noah snatched it out of the computer and slipped it into his pocket. He was retrieving another identical device to try to use on one of the other computers when his phone vibrated in his pocket. He checked it and saw a new voicemail had come in.

Winter.

He navigated to the voicemail and put the phone near his ear. *"I don't know how much longer I can do this... Um, I'm okay. Sorry to bother you. I just wanted to hear your voice. See you at five."*

Noah's blood boiled, and his fingers tightened. There was

that catch in her voice that told him, right now, she needed him. And that was very special because his fiercely independent wife only let that slip that only once in a blue moon.

He was about to sprint out the back to be by her side when Winter's phone pinged with another message. Another restricted number, or maybe the same one. No text this time. Just a picture—Winter wearing the exact clothes he'd dropped her off in, glancing over her shoulder as she walked into Cumberland.

29

On Monday, Winter showed up for work in her Honda Pilot an hour late. She was dressed in casual, unrevealing clothes—proper climbing pants, a black t-shirt, and boots. To this she added her favorite accessory, her gun, which she'd tucked under her hip-length jacket. She wore her hair back in a ponytail and had smeared on a bit of tinted sunscreen but was otherwise makeup free. She looked like she would any other day.

She'd spent the night agonizing about how to handle Nathan Lynch. She tried to talk herself into continuing with the role she'd drawn for herself, to figure out how she could endure another day, another minute, another second of that sleazy rich boy putting his tentacles all over her.

It was a nightmare that jogged her back to her senses. Feeling trapped inside her own body, her eyes forced open like *A Clockwork Orange* as images flashed on a silver screen. Her baby brother laughing, pouting, screaming. Drugging her and beating her into submission. Dyeing her hair.

The unmistakable sound of duct tape as she bound Greg and Andrea Stewart to chairs inside the RV. The cinch of tape around Timothy's little wrists. Thirteen-year-old Nicole Stewart screaming as Justin pressed his body against hers, a gun to her head, and told her to choose which of her parents should die first.

"You have to accept things in life for what they are. Not what you want them to be." Justin's eyes slid to Winter so she would know he was talking to her too.

The crack of bone ringing in her ears like the blast of a shotgun. Justin biting the corner of his lip as he forced Winter to kill first the dad, then the mom. Then Nicole died, too, with a bullet in her brain.

Blood spattered her face. Eight-year-old Timothy Stewart's muffled screams rang in her ears.

Winter crashed through the front door of Cumberland, not giving two shits about any of the eyes that lifted to look at her. To hell with all the dancing around. She couldn't take another minute of it.

Nathan Lynch was nothing compared to some of the hideous excuses for humanity she'd been forced to endure over the years. She was done degrading herself to try to finesse information out of him. She would break his arm to get him to tell her the truth and then deal with the consequences.

Hopefully, he wouldn't push her that far.

The office was a ghost town.

She walked up to Dawn at the desk. A sign was set up on her counter, letting employees know that they were all going to be interviewed by the police and would be expected to report to the conference room when called.

After Winter tore Nathan Lynch a brand-new asshole, she'd do all the interviewing they wanted.

As she signed her name, she looked at the ones crossed off above hers. Nathan Lynch's was not. "Dawn, is Nathan—"

"Getting interviewed again by the police? Yes, he's in there now." The young woman gave her a doe-eyed look.

Dammit!

Winter had enough energy to fuel a rocket to the moon, and no Nathan Lynch to release it on.

She looked up at the climbing wall, then back at the receptionist. "Um, Dawn?"

"Yeah?"

"You still got a pair of size nine climbing shoes back there?"

"Sure do!"

Ten minutes later, not bothering to knock, Winter threw open the door of Nathan Lynch's office, stomped inside, and slammed it closed.

Lynch startled at the abrupt intrusion. He was pacing in front of his desk, phone to his ear. His eyes swept over her, taking in her abrupt change of appearance with an expected amount of disdain.

"I'll call you back." He slid the phone away from his ear. "Feeling eager this morning, hmm?"

Winter took a deep breath through her nostrils, grounding herself to the spot.

"Didn't Melissa have a conversation with you about our dress code? Especially for salespeople, it's important to represent the values of the company."

"Shut up, Nathan."

His eyes widened, but he laughed through the awkwardness. "Excuse me?"

"It's over. Do you understand? You've had your fun and now playtime is at an end."

"Are you threatening me, Samantha?" He still looked vaguely aroused.

"You're damn right, I am. I know what you've been doing. I know about the cameras."

The change in his expression from cocksure to concerned was so subtle, she might not have seen it if she weren't staring quite so hard. "What cameras?"

A flick of his eye was all it took. Winter looked over her shoulder at the square whiteboard hanging from the opposite wall. She went to it and yanked it off, revealing a wall safe with a faint red glow all around it. All at once, she knew she'd found his cache of trophies. The red glow never led her astray.

"What the hell do you think you're doing?" At last, he was taking her seriously, anger rising in his voice. He reached out like he might grab her. "Get away from there!"

Winter whirled on him, flicking back her jacket so he got a clear view of the gun on her hip.

Lynch's reaching hand froze in midair.

"If you touch me, ever again, I'm going to fuck up all that pretty dental work of yours."

Just as she'd seen the other day when Melissa had shown interest in another man, the mask of his face shifted. His eyes darkened, and his lips went flat. "Who the hell are you?"

"My name is Winter Black. I'm former FBI, now a private investigator. Helen hired me to get enough dirt on you to put you away for the sick things you've done to her and every other woman in this office."

He clenched his teeth like an animal but retreated a step. "This is horseshit. You've been spying on me."

"That's rich." Winter lifted her eyebrows. "I bet you have cameras in the conference room, too, considering how many women you've forced to spend time with you in there. Are you recording police interviews right now? Are you sure that's legal?"

"Helen is dead." Nathan tilted his head to one side, cockiness creeping back in. "So what the hell exactly are you still doing here?"

"That's none of your business. If I were you, I'd be worried more about myself."

"You've got nothing." His gaze flicked to the safe. "And you don't have the right to open that or search my property or anything."

"True enough. But what you don't know about is all the evidence I've already collected. All it takes is one little phone call to the media, and they'll be swarming this place, making it hard for the rangers and the police and the FBI to do their work. With one person missing and others murdered, they're looking for an excuse to dig deeper into you."

Nathan appeared unmoved.

Winter saturated her next words with scorn. "Considering the kind of scrutiny you'll be under, do you think you'll be able to keep your deviant behavior a secret? And when they find out what you're capable of, you're going to become a prime suspect."

He laughed again, defensively. "I have solid alibis. You can't pin any of that shit on me."

"Maybe not, but the damage to your reputation would be irreversible. Not to mention, I already have everything I need to make one very interesting phone call to your wife."

"You wouldn't dare…" A quiver flecked each word. Now he was terrified. And for the very first time, she wondered if his alibis was actually legit.

"You're going to cooperate fully with my investigation and give me everything I need, including turning over all the photos and video you've collected over the years."

"Why? So you can destroy me with it?" His mouth twisted into a snarl. "You rancid bitch!"

"So I can use it to catch the killer, Nathan." Winter dropped her hand from her hip, allowing her leather jacket to cover the gun once again. "And you'll keep my true identity to yourself. Unless you want your wife, and every news outlet I can think of, to get one hell of a graphic email."

His lower lip trembled. And she watched him crack like an egg smacked by a frying pan. "You can't tell my wife. Please. You can't. I'll do whatever you say."

"That's more like it." Winter jutted out her chin, the warm tingles of victory crackling across her skin. "Now be a good boy—"

A sharp knock at the door cut her off.

Winter drew back just as it was thrown open to reveal a man with dark skin and a broad nose looking at her with a deeply unimpressed expression.

"Winter Black…" Detective Darnell Davenport spoke her name like a curse.

She exhaled sharply, realizing she'd barely gotten in under the wire with telling Lynch the truth. "Nice to see you, too, Darnell."

He pinched the bridge of his nose and looked down. "You here to make my life a living hell the rest of the week? Month? Year? How much of this do I have to endure this time?"

"I thought the FBI was handling this case?"

"The jurisdiction on this one is complicated. PD will be conducting the rest of the interviews through tomorrow."

"You looking to talk to Nathan again?" She regarded him like spilled milk curdling in the sun. "I'm done with him for now."

Darnell shook his tired, irritated head.

It was such a shame their at-first-promising working relationship had ended up so sour. She'd gotten too close one too many times. Made far too many headaches for Darnell and essentially used up all her goodwill currency with the Austin PD. Last time they spoke, he'd given her a lecture about not understanding the line between the private sector and law enforcement. The look on his face said he was gearing up for the exact same lecture now.

"What the hell are you doing here?" he demanded.

"I'd rather tell you during my scheduled interview, if you don't mind. I'm officially on the Cumberland payroll, after all."

"Of course you are. I'm not handling the interviews." He rolled his eyes so hard, they looked like they might fall out. Still, he quickly shifted his attention to Nathan Lynch. "I need to ask, do you have any information on the whereabouts of Melissa Hinds?"

"No. Why?"

Clearly, Nathan was feeling less loquacious than usual. Winter couldn't imagine why.

"She's not here. Did you not notice?" Darnell sneered. "She's not responding to calls. An officer stopped by her house, and she didn't answer the door."

"You think something happened to her? Like the others?"

Nathan, in all his tanned glory, had never looked paler, and Winter was shocked by the genuine concern in his voice.

"We have a BOLO out on her. Officers are headed there now to conduct an official wellness check and will forcibly gain entry to confirm she's alive." Darnell's eyes swept over Nathan Lynch, then came to land on Winter, where they narrowed into slits. "You're next, Winter. And this had better be good." The detective shot back out the door as abruptly as he'd entered.

Winter was on his heels when she remembered she had one more thing to tell Nathan Lynch.

She turned and strutted back into his office, pulling the tiny red flag from a back pocket. "Here's your hankie," she said, slamming it into his chest. "Sorry to break up the boys club."

30

Noah knew exactly where he could find Eve at one thirty on a Monday. Monday was two-for-one dim sum day at Kung Po Kitchen in downtown Austin, which Eve went to great lengths to attend, grumbling for at least a week whenever work or anything else forced her to miss it.

He stepped through the swinging doors into the cool of the dining room. On the far wall was a series of large aquarium tanks stacked one on top of the other, containing strange and hideous fish that would be chopped up and eaten throughout the day. His eyes scanned the tables, occupied mostly by Chinese people and people of Chinese descent, and paused at one bright-blond ponytail near the back.

His body was twitching with stress—like steam building up inside a kettle—but all that energy needed to be saved for later. Right now, he had to be cool.

Putting his shoulders back and forcing a perfectly casual demeanor—just another day on the beat—Noah approached.

When Eve spotted him, she froze, a steamed pork bun clenched between her chopsticks a few inches from her mouth. She grimaced, her cheeks puffing in disapproval, before shoving the whole thing into her mouth.

"This seat taken?" Noah set his hand on the back of a rickety chair and pulled it out. He sat down, the wood creaking under his weight.

"I old ou no o all me…" She spoke through the oversize *baozi*.

"Exactly. That's why I didn't call. And I didn't think you'd appreciate me showing up at the office."

She swallowed, then took a pull of water from her plastic straw. "Falkner's about three seconds from skinning you alive and using the leather to reupholster his office chair."

"That's unnecessarily graphic." Noah plucked an egg custard tart from her plate and took a bite. "His words or yours?"

"*His*, Noah." She drummed her chopsticks on the side of the plate. *Tink, tink, tink.* "I haven't told him about Winter's involvement in the Parker Roy case. He will shit a brick when he finds out. *If* he finds out."

"Why wouldn't he find out?"

"Well, he doesn't review every single case himself. The FBI is just consulting, so Winter's dealing more with APD and the parks department. I thought maybe if I kept my mouth shut, I'd save both of you the trouble this could inevitably cause."

"I really do appreciate that." Noah caught her eyes, his lips pulling into a sincere smile. "But that isn't what I wanted to talk to you about."

"Of course not. You want to talk to me about that plate you had me run."

"Well…"

"I told you." She plucked a dumpling off her plate with her chopsticks. "I can't be involved in this. In spite of how much I bitch and moan, I actually like my job, and I want to keep it." Eve popped the dumpling into her mouth.

"Carl Gardner is the one…or *one* of the ones…who's been stalking Winter. Sending her text messages, filming her at the office. Even at Cumberland."

Eve swallowed. "Son of a…" She set an elbow on the table, then let her head rest on her hand.

"Gardner's working with Justin's fan club. I don't think he's the main guy behind everything. But this isn't his end game. They're planning something. Something to do with Winter. They're following her. It's only a matter of time."

"I can't help you. You're gonna have to go to Weston."

He scoffed so hard it hurt his throat. "You mean the guy who wants to skin me alive?"

"He's a professional. He knows how serious the situation with Justin is. He'd never leave you flailing on your own."

"And when he finds out I've been moonlighting to follow this case?"

"You're the victim here. What would anybody expect you to do? It's not like you've been flashing your badge…" She trailed off, scrutinizing every twitch of his face. "Holy shit, you have been, haven't you?"

"I will do whatever I have to do to protect Winter."

She sighed loudly and cracked her neck, like a football player in pregame. "If you have proof Justin is in any way involved in this—"

"I do. Maybe not Justin himself, but someone who sees themselves as his 'right hand.'"

"Then we have to go to Weston. Justin's crimes, including his cybercrimes, cross state and even international lines. It's an FBI matter."

He sucked in a breath for rebuttal.

"You said you'd do anything you had to in order to protect Winter. And going to Weston is your best chance."

Noah held the breath for a second, then sighed it out. "Dammit."

"Send me everything you have so far, and I'll take it to him. He'll have a better attitude about the whole thing if it comes from me." She pointed her chopsticks at him. "But before I do that, you need to tell me anything illegal you might've done to obtain your evidence."

Another painful scoff. "I'd rather not."

"I'm aware of that."

He drummed his fingers on the sticky tabletop. "Will you tell Falkner?"

Eve's eyes drifted to the tanks, and they both watched a cook wrangle out a particularly hideous fish that splashed and thrashed through its final moments. "I'll tell him everything he needs to know for us to work the case and protect Winter." Her gaze flicked back to his. "First, you need to tell me the truth."

31

Based on his scowl and his short, clipped sentences, Winter knew just how excited Darnell was to see her at Cumberland. He'd grilled her twice, then stared at her like a mosquito he wanted to squash.

But he hadn't told her to back off, hadn't insisted the situation was too dangerous, hadn't threatened to expose her. He accepted the situation as he would a throbbing pain in his neck that needed to be iced, then sent her out the door with a flick of his exasperated wrist.

Good enough, Winter figured. But she reckoned it might be best to stay out of his way for a little while. So although she was scheduled for an all-day shift at Cumberland, she decided to clock off early and head back to her own office.

Before she left, Winter had made a quick search of the ladies' restrooms and locker rooms, sketching out the location of no less than a dozen cameras. Many of them were mounted very low, the angle pointing up. Others were placed high above, maybe to look down blouses.

She wanted to find all the cameras in Nathan Lynch's office but decided to go after that unfortunate task another time. She couldn't stand to be in the same room with the man for another second. Besides, what she'd taken was likely more than enough to prove Helen's sexual harassment case.

The events of the morning had left her more confused than before. Ever since Helen walked into her office, Winter had been convinced that Nathan Lynch was the big bad in all this. The kidnapper and the killer. He'd already proven himself a creep. She was almost positive he was a rapist as well.

Lynch needed to be taken down and dragged through the dirt, even do some prison time for his crimes. But his demeanor wasn't stacking up with what she expected from this killer, especially the way he responded to the prospect of his wife discovering his extramarital dalliances.

If she assumed his alibis were solid, then he wasn't the killer. It was time she and everyone else began exploring other possibilities.

If Tucker Hicks were still alive, he would've been the next obvious suspect. Nobody else in the office stood out. Perhaps she'd just been too focused on Nathan to really see anybody else.

When she arrived at her office, Ariel was at her desk tapping away. She smiled as she greeted Winter.

She wished she could let her guard down, but with everything Noah had been learning about the person or persons who were following her, she was on edge. She could never relax, not fully. Her nerves were always pulled too tight.

Part of her wanted to simply confront Ariel about Noah's suspicions. Ask her point blank how she knew Carl Gardner. Or maybe go the long way around to the question, disguising her inquiries as girl talk. *Noah saw you talking to some guy at Duncan Brothers the other day...were you on a date?*

Before she could decide on which approach to take, her

phone vibrated in her pocket with an incoming call. Very few people had the number, so it was safe to assume it was either Noah or someone from Cumberland…

Nathan Lynch's private extension populated the screen.

Winter breezed by Ariel and into her office, then drew the privacy blinds before she answered.

"What?"

"I have a proposal for you." His voice had regained its cool confidence.

"Have you come to your senses and decided to hand over all the videos you've taken of your employees?"

"I never once took leave of my senses." She could hear the smirk in his voice. "After having endured a third round of questioning by the authorities, my lawyer and I are getting the impression my alibis aren't strong enough to prove my innocence. But that's neither here nor there. What matters is protecting my employees and getting justice for those who've been harmed."

"Mm-hmm…"

"I've been running a check of your background, former FBI Special Agent Winter Black, and I have to say I'm impressed."

"Gee."

"Helen always had a good head on her shoulders, and it seems she made a wise choice in picking her P.I."

"You realize Helen hired me to investigate your wrongdoings, right?"

"That was a misguided waste of money."

Winter slapped her sketch of camera locations on the desk. "I'm not so sure."

"Take a step back, Miss Black, and consider the situation from another angle."

"*Miss* Black? That tall hunk of good-looking man isn't my brother. He's my husband. You were saying?

Lynch cleared his throat. "I'm offering to pay your retainer."

"What?" She had to sit down. "Why?"

"Given their fixation on me, I'm not confident the police are properly handling this case. Tucker was my friend, and while I can't say the same for Parker or Helen, or Aliyah for that matter, I still want to know what happened to them. More than that, I'm concerned about my own safety."

Aliyah was still missing. Just hours shy of a week in the wilderness, injured, terrified, starving—and that was if she was still alive. But the rangers were doing all they could. And SARs had helicopters circling, along with teams on foot.

Winter turned her sketch over absently in her hands. "I am incredulous that a man like you would hire any woman to be his protector."

"This is far from the only precaution I'll be taking. I've already sent my wife and children to stay with my in-laws in Plano until the killer's found. And my house is armed with a state-of-the-art security system. I've also decided to hire my own guard to watch the gate."

"That sounds marginally sufficient."

"Come and work for me, and I'll make it worth your while…"

"Stop right there, Nathan. I cannot be bought. I don't care how much money you offer me."

"You're an investigator for hire, aren't you?" A snotty, rich-man chuckle pierced her ear. "That categorically means you can be bought. All I want you to do is what you've been doing. Continue pretending to be an employee and keep track of everything that happens around the office. Unlike the police, the killer has no reason to be overly cautious around you and might reveal himself."

"You know what I think?" Winter set the camera down and sat up straight in her chair. "I think you just want to hire me as a PR stunt, so when this whole thing's over, you can point to me and say you did everything you could."

"I won't deny that factored into my thinking. Must I be persecuted for being thorough?"

"No, there are other reasons you deserve to be persecuted. Or prosecuted for that matter."

"I'm worried about Melissa too." He let out an affected sigh. "I feel like the authorities aren't taking her disappearance seriously enough, given the circumstances."

She narrowed her gaze suspiciously. "What do you care about Melissa?"

"I just want to make sure she's safe. Does that make me a terrible person?"

It doesn't make you not *a terrible person.*

Still, his offer did give Winter pause. If he was the killer, why would he want a private investigator lurking around his hunting grounds? Unless this was an extreme and grandiose case of the killer trying to involve themselves in the investigation as a way to divert suspicion. Such actions on the part of criminals often led to their arrest. Police had been wise to that game since at least the eighteen hundreds.

She wasn't remotely convinced he cared about anything other than protecting his own ass, but taking him on as a client meant she'd still have unfettered access to Cumberland. It also meant she could continue to be paid for her efforts, which was never a bad thing. And when the time came, she could feed him to the wolves if need be.

"All right. I'll play. But I have some conditions."

"Shoot."

"First, I need you to commit to cleaning up your behavior. No more office dalliances. No more late nights alone with anyone. And if you even think about laying a finger on me, I will show you just how capable I am of protecting myself."

"I think that goes without saying."

Winter tented her fingers on her desk. "You'll also need to maintain my cover. I need a different job, something that allows me to wander the building at my discretion without arousing suspicion."

"Hmm. Well, I could make you a personal assistant. Since we lost Tucker, Bryan has more or less taken over HR until we're able to hire someone. You can cover his duties."

Bryan. She'd almost forgotten about him—Christina's mourning boyfriend with the sad eyes.

"That works." Winter nodded. "I'll be in tomorrow."

"Excellent. What time can I expect you?"

Winter hung up and tossed her phone on the desk. She'd take his money, play his little game. But she'd be damned if she'd ever answer to that man.

32

A timid knock came at Winter's office door.

"Come in."

The door creaked open, and Ariel stepped inside, her eyes wide and sparkling with concern. Winter knew that little chipmunk look. Ariel had a question she wanted to ask, something that was making her nervous. Normally, this aroused nothing more than tepid curiosity in Winter, but she couldn't stop thinking about what Noah had told her.

Once again, she almost blurted it out. *Have you been spying on me? Are you one of them?*

"I wasn't trying to eavesdrop..." Ariel tucked a wild curl behind one nearly circular, sticky-outie ear. "But was that Nathan Lynch on the phone?"

Didn't mean to eavesdrop. What a load. "Why do you ask?" Winter gestured to the chair in front of her desk with an open palm.

Ariel sat down. "Dang it. Okay. Well, promise you won't get mad?"

"No, but continue."

"Well, I sorta kinda flirted with one of the dudes down at the records office."

"Ariel," Winter admonished playfully.

"He told me how much Nathan Lynch paid Parker Roy when they settled out of court."

"Oooh. Okay, I'm not mad."

Again, Ariel checked over her shoulders. "Eighty thousand dollars."

"Really?"

"So I'm asking myself, why would Lynch give him so much money?"

"To shut him up."

She nodded, her whole body bouncing in her chair. "And I'm wondering, has he ever paid off anybody else? And I did find a case that was filed right around the same time he stepped down at Carmean. The plaintiff was a woman named Camille DiSanto. She claimed her boss offered her a promotion if she slept with him."

Winter pinched the bridge of her nose. "And what happened?"

"She did it, and he didn't give her the promotion, so she filed suit against the company. Or at least, that's what I was able to figure."

"Did Carmean pay her off?"

"It was settled out of court."

"He's a serial abuser, that's for sure. I think he's a rapist too. He uses these companies as his personal little playgrounds, then when he gets in trouble, he ponies up the hush money and goes dark for a while to let things cool down."

Ariel shuddered. "A corporate sleazeball rapist."

"That sums it up." Winter drummed her fingers on her desk, thinking. "Unfortunately, he's not stupid. He knows everything at Cumberland's about to blow up. He's trying to redirect my attention away from him and toward the murders so he can hop a private jet to Morocco or some other country that doesn't have an extradition agreement with the U.S. And quietly wait for the statute of limitations of run out."

"So you don't think he's the killer anymore?"

"No, I don't." She sighed with just how irritating that fact was. "But he's still a predator. And it is still my job to make sure he pays for what he's done."

"If the killer doesn't get to him first."

Winter's face pinched at the comment. Nathan had expressed the exact same concern. If he wasn't the killer, then he was on the killer's list of victims. But why?

She dragged her gaze slowly back to Ariel, a knowing smirk tugging on her lips. The girl didn't look it, what with her pink, glitter-tipped nails, perfectly tousled curls, and big bush baby eyes, but she had the makings of a fine investigator.

Or actress.

"If we're going to catch this guy before he kills again, we need to figure out why he started killing in the first place."

"The million-dollar question."

"Parker Roy, Aliyah Andry, Helen Marchland, Tucker Hicks." Winter ticked the names off on her fingers. "All these people had something in common, something more than simply working at Cumberland. The manner of killing, the choice of victims, the sentimental dumping ground. There's nothing random about these murders. And all these people shared a common enemy, which, at a glance, is Nathan Lynch."

"But if he's not the killer…" Ariel's eyes went even wider.

"Right, then who?"

33

Now that I'd had a chance to practice my design on a few live models, I realized some of the knots could be tied beforehand. That way, I could slip my victim inside quick, like putting on a shirt, then drive the knots down tight to immediately establish complete control, just in case they came to before they were secured.

I drew the rope over my hands, plaiting in another slipknot. What would my old man say when he woke up caught in my webs? Because I wouldn't gag him like the others. I was going to listen to every word that came out of his filthy mouth. This man who used to be a monolith in my eyes—I'd break him into tiny pieces. Break his spirit. I was going to make him cry as the tears streamed down, just like he always did to me.

Like he always did to my mother. One time, he couldn't take the sound of her crying anymore, so he cut her with a paring knife. And kept cutting her 'til our kitchen was covered in blood, and she finally held her tongue.

He thought he'd caged her so she could never escape. But

she took the same way out that any truly virtuous woman would. *The same escape you took, Christina.*

My hands clenched tight, then grew weak. I dropped the ropes at my feet. Hot tears burned the back of my eyes. I pressed my fingers over them and sucked a breath through my teeth.

"No more tears. Not from me." I stood and began to pace between the piles of file boxes and office supplies that littered the storeroom. Piles upon piles of organized clutter.

The time had come. I'd drawn this out long enough. Two more names on my list. I'd meant to go in order, but I couldn't risk it. All the scrutiny raining down on the company, the police everywhere. They'd catch on to me soon if I didn't get out.

And they were definitely going to catch on to him. His feet were nearly as itchy as mine right now, ready to skip town and be done with all this. The difference was, he'd be able to come back in a few years smelling like roses. Whereas I would be destroyed.

I couldn't let that happen. The murder of the people responsible for Christina's death was my magnum opus, and I would finish it.

The only hiccup was Melissa. She was supposed to die first.

First her, then the man who killed you, and then last of all, the man who killed my mother.

I had to make my move and get out quickly. The thought of being caught was worse than the sound of wolves creeping up while I slept naked in the woods. But leaving my work unfinished—I couldn't let that happen.

My father and the man who killed you are cut from the same cloth. Destroyers of women. Monsters who think they're above punishment. I was born to bring them back down to earth and bury them.

But Melissa. Melissa. She was missing. The police thought I'd taken her. God knew I would've, given the chance.

It wasn't the first time she'd taken a personal day after taking a good-time pounding. I'd been sitting here in this very room with Tucker's body beside me starting to stink. I would've gotten him out sooner, but Melissa stayed late. Not to work. I wasn't even sure she knew how to work, as all she ever seemed to do was lie on her back with her legs spread open.

I walked to the wall and pulled aside a box where I could peek through the hole. I'd drilled it in exactly this spot because I'd already known his pattern, the places in his office he most liked to take them—the couch on the southern wall and his desk. He had no idea I was watching him, of course. Well, watching her. Whoever she happened to be.

When he bent Melissa over the desk, yanking both her arms hard behind her and holding them like she was cuffed, her eyes had been pointed right at me. I almost thought she saw me. Like she was looking right into my eyes as he destroyed her body, used her in whatever way he pleased.

Melissa never fought back. He was so rough with her that night, so angry. He held her down, spanked her, slapped her face, choked her. Made her beg for more. And when he was done, he told her what a good girl she was. And she laughed like he'd just told her a joke.

And it reminded me of you.

That day in the woods when you laughed at me. I was trying to tell you how much I loved you, but the words came out wrong. And you laughed. Right there in our special spot.

I was here in the storeroom the first night he made you stay. I was going to save you from him. I was going to help you. And I would've helped you, but you didn't fight back.

I was going to marry you. I would've treated you so well, so much better than my father treated my mother.

But you didn't fight back.

I thought you were too good for this world, too delicate. But you didn't fight back that first night with him. Or the second. Or the third. You never fought back.

The man who broke you was going to die today.

Circumstance was forcing me to hurry along my plans, but there was no force in this world that could stop me from taking my time with him.

My life had been leading up to this moment.

34

Winter lifted her gaze as someone approached the office. Her muscles barely had time to tighten before she recognized Noah.

Her husband was a lot of things, but delicate wasn't one of them. The moment he stepped inside, he was probably going to demand Ariel provide an explanation for her meeting with Carl Gardner. Winter's opportunity to beat him to it was rapidly closing.

She flicked her gaze to Ariel, who'd risen from her seat and was headed out of Winter's office back toward her desk.

"Hang on a sec."

Ariel turned, her eager smile never fading. "What's up?"

"I need to ask you about something."

"Okay." She pushed a strand of hair behind her ear and faced the desk.

"How do you know Carl Gardner?"

It was subtle, but Ariel's eyes widened in recognition, confirming everything Noah had said.

Noah had made his way from the street into Winter's office. He seemed to assess what was happening and paused in the doorway, throwing up an arm on the jamb. Then he put on his incredibly intimidating interrogation face and stared at Ariel like she was a terrorist who'd been caught in the act.

There was no way out.

"I'm not accusing you of anything." Winter rose from her seat and stepped around her desk to look her in the eye. "Not yet. But I need answers. Have you been spying on me?"

"What?" Ariel's face paled. "No! Of course not."

"Then why are you having coffee dates with a man who is?" Noah's voice boomed through the tiny office.

Ariel did a double take—Noah, Winter, Noah, Winter. "I don't know what you're talking about. He's not spying. He's just trying to do research for his book."

"His book?" he barked.

Winter shot Noah a look. "Why don't you start at the beginning?"

Ariel covered her face with her hands, her shoulders shaking. After a few long moments, she took a deep breath and forced herself to look up. "He contacted me a few weeks ago."

Noah took a heavy step forward. "How?"

"On the phone."

"Office or private?"

"Private. He said he was writing a case study on The Preacher. He just wanted to ask me some questions, get my take on it."

"Why didn't he contact Winter directly?"

"Because I told him not to." She lifted her big eyes to Winter. "I didn't want him to bother you. So I agreed to meet him and give him an interview instead."

"Why didn't you tell me about this?"

"I didn't want to trigger you. You have PTSD. You shouldn't have to think about that stuff."

Winter's heart pinched. She balled her hands into fists. "I don't need you to protect me. I need you to be honest with me. I told you that when I hired you."

"I'm sorry." Again, she hung her head in her hands. "I just…I thought I could handle it. Get rid of him for you. Show you that I'm cut out to be a real partner." Her voice broke with a little sob, but she held it back. "I swear, I didn't tell him anything he couldn't have found online anyway. All I know about The Preacher is what I've read."

"He's not a writer, and he doesn't give a damn about The Preacher." Noah hadn't softened at all. "He's the one who's been stalking Winter. One of Justin's freakish fans."

"Are you serious?" Ariel paled further still, and her mouth dropped open. "I didn't know. I swear I didn't know."

"Some P.I."

Winter walked over and laid her hand lightly on her husband's forearm. "Did he ever ask for any personal details on me?"

"I…I guess. He asked about your schedule. He kept wanting to find time for an interview with you. He also asked about some personal stuff."

Noah growled. "Like what?"

"How she took her coffee. Where she likes to have lunch. I thought it was kind of weird, but he said he wanted to craft an authentic narrative." Suddenly, Ariel slapped herself in the forehead. "God, I'm so stupid! I'm sorry, Winter. I was just trying to help."

"I believe you."

Ariel and Noah both looked fixedly at Winter, one with an expression of hope and the other bordering on calling her an idiot.

"I don't think you'd ever hurt me on purpose."

"I wouldn't. I swear. Winter, you mean so much to me…"

Noah's phone began to ring with the special tone he used

for Eve, "Poker Face" by Lady Gaga. It was a private joke between them that Winter didn't really understand. Something about bamboo.

He stepped out the door before answering, "Got something good for me?"

Winter turned her attention back to Ariel. "I can't work with you if I can't trust you."

"I know." Ariel was crying now, though she was fighting to wipe back all the tears before they touched her cheeks.

A part of Winter wanted to pat her back and tell it that it was okay.

She didn't move.

"Because of Justin Black and Douglas Kilroy, I'll always have people who are interested in me, who want to hurt me. That means, if anybody ever calls you asking about me or claims to know someone I know or wants to write about me, even if it's just an online review, I need to know about it."

"I understand. I promise I will never, ever try to hide anything from you ever again. I'm so sorry."

Noah entered and pocketed his phone as he hurried back to Winter. "Falkner okayed a raid on Gardner's office. He's letting me join in. I'm officially off leave."

"That's excellent news."

"Well." His lips pulled hard to one side. "I'm back on leave as soon as the raid's over, but at least he's not trying to keep me out."

"Probably because he knows you'll just show up and join in anyway."

"That's my reputation these days, ain't it?" Noah scratched the back of his neck. "Dammit. Oh, well. Worked in my favor this time."

"You always find a way." Winter stepped up close, set her hand on his cheek, and went on her tiptoes to kiss him. "Be careful. I mean it."

"I will." He gave Ariel one last death stare—his silent warning that if she ever hurt Winter again, he might just kidnap her and leave her lost in the middle of the desert. With a grunt, he gave Winter one more kiss and was out the door without another word.

35

At eight o'clock on the dot, Noah, Eve, and two other agents from the Violent Crime Unit arrived at the warehouse where Carl Gardner had his office. After digging into it, Eve had concluded that this was his home address as well. That fit with what Noah had seen inside.

The piles of dishes and empty chip bags. The smell of rank humanity. Carl lived most of his life in that dark little room.

Noah was relieved to discover Ariel had not willfully betrayed them. Not because he gave a crap about her, but because of what it would've done to his wife to learn she'd picked the wrong person to trust. Again.

Noah checked his weapon and geared up—bulletproof vest, FBI jacket, shoulder mic to coordinate the raid. It all itched at the red patch that spread across his shoulders and along his neck.

The doctor he'd talked to online said the itchiness was just hives brought about by stress. She prescribed a cream, but also said the only real cure was to reduce stress.

He hadn't meant to laugh in her virtual face, but he did.

Before heading in, Eve and the two other agents accompanying them got together to discuss their strategy. As they talked, Noah came to an uncomfortable realization. He worked within a stone's throw of both of these men, and he didn't know either of their names.

He'd never asked.

Back in Richmond, he'd made a point of knowing everybody in the building, from the kids who worked in the cafeteria to the uniformed cop who guarded the door.

Maybe Weston Falkner had a point. He'd been taking his job lightly. He wasn't treating the Bureau with the deference it deserved. By now, he should've known so much more about the other agents he worked with than just their names. And he didn't even have those.

"Dalton and I will start in the front and head for the computer room," Eve said. "Muñoz, you and Ross come from the back and secure the perimeter."

Muñoz and Ross, Noah repeated in his head. *Muñoz and Ross.*

Quickly, the four of them got into position. Noah and Eve went to the door he'd busted open previously. A new door had been installed. Eve pounded on it with her fist.

"FBI! Open up!"

She tried the handle, and to Noah's surprise, it swung right open.

It was like Carl Gardner wanted to get himself caught. Or someone did.

As they stepped inside, Eve radioed the other team, coordinating their positions. They moved down the hall with weapons drawn until they came to Carl Gardner's office. Amazingly, impossibly, the door still hung wide open.

Eve and Noah did a quick check of the room. Then she headed straight for the computers. He drew her attention toward one monitor in particular, the one displaying a running feed from Justin's fan club. Today, it was open to a chatroom called *The Darkening Storm*.

The most recent comment was written by username *jb4prez*. *We have to be patient, but we must also pave the way and remove all obstacles. Justin started all these years ago when he first drenched his hands in blood. We will be the ones to finish it.*

Eve made a weird groaning noise Noah had never heard come out of her before. "What in the name of...?"

"There's a whole community of them." Noah rested his gloved hand on the back of the chair and leaned toward the screen. "They're obsessed with Justin. Like he's the second coming or some shit."

"Looks to me like they're getting ready for a third."

Suddenly, the screen blurred into pixelated white lines.

"Shit!" Eve pushed back from the table. "Someone's burning out the drive!"

"They know we're here."

The crack of the gunshot hit even as the computer box on the desk exploded. Gun in hand, Noah whipped around to find Carl Gardner standing in the doorway, a pistol in his grip. With a hand on the butt to steady his aim, Gardner fired again. The bullet missed Eve by an inch as another computer box exploded.

Noah took aim carefully but quickly and did not hesitate to squeeze the trigger.

Blood burst from Gardner's stomach, and he went down.

Noah rushed closer, kicking Gardner's gun away before crouching at his side. Blood was on his lips, and he'd broken his glasses when he fell. He twitched, voice arrested so he barely even moaned in pain.

In the background, Eve called for emergency services and reported to the other team.

"Idiot." Noah put pressure on the wound. He'd hit him a few inches up and to one side of his belly button. Blood pulsed and oozed from the hole. "What did you think was gonna happen if you opened fire on federal agents?"

He went into his belt and yanked out his compact trauma kit. Ripping open the packet with his teeth, he poured coagulating solution on the wound. He unpacked a tightly folded square of thick gauze and pressed it down firmly.

"Don't die, you little bastard. I need to talk to you."

Gardner looked at Noah and blinked slowly. The recognition was there on his face, just as before. A tortured squeak parted his lips.

"You're dead." Before he could say more, his eyes rolled back, and he fell unconscious.

36

Winter stood off to one side of Nathan Lynch's desk so her back wouldn't be to the door. Just being around him made her muscles tense and threw her hypervigilance into high gear.

She drummed her fingertips on her crossed arms. "I'm going to need access to all your HR files."

"Whatever you think's necessary." He smirked and tossed his water bottle from one hand to the other. His cheeks looked flushed, capillaries broken under the skin. She wondered if he'd been drinking last night, trying to cope with his whole life crumbling around him.

The phone on his desk rang. He held one finger out to Winter. "This is Nathan…yes, of course. Put him through." He glanced up at her. "I've got to take this."

"You said Bryan was going to be coming in to show me the ropes."

"Yes, but he's also filling in for Tucker. Go talk to him yourself…" He shooed her out with a wave of the hand. "What's up, Robbins? I hear you're ready to get your ass kicked on the pickleball court again."

Yeah, that sounds urgent.

Was there anything more vomit-inducing than corporate bro culture? Winter couldn't think of anything other than actual vomit.

Rolling her eyes, she turned on a heel and walked out. The less time she had to spend around him, the better. Having him dislike her was so much more pleasant than the alternative.

She moved down the hall to the HR office—Tucker's old office.

The door was open a crack, but Winter still knocked politely before stepping in. "Bryan?"

The smell of Tucker's cologne still lingered in the air. The desk was empty, but as her gaze drifted across the room, she focused on Bryan sitting in his office chair by the window. He was just staring outside. Except there was something in his hands he seemed to be fiddling with. His back was to Winter, so she couldn't see what it was.

"Bryan?" Winter inched over the threshold. "Are you okay?"

He didn't move. Assuming he had headphones on, Winter made a wide circle to approach him, coming into his periphery first so she wouldn't startle him.

Nobody liked to be startled. It was common courtesy.

As she moved closer, she saw nothing in his ears. A two- or three-day beard grew on his chin, his brown hair askew. His face held a grimace chiseled in stone. Fluffy clouds outside the window reflected in his eyes like mirrors. His hands were empty, but they moved quick and light, as if he held something in them.

"Bryan?" Very slowly, Winter reached out to set the tips of her fingers on his shoulder. He flinched, and she pulled back. "I'm sorry. I didn't mean to startle you. Are you okay?"

He craned his neck to look up at her, then wheeled his

chair back from the glass and stood. "Oh, hi, Sam." Shaking his head, he ran a hand through his messy hair. "Sorry. I was really zoning out there."

She chuckled lightly to cut the tension. "No problem. Is everything okay?"

"No, actually. It's my father. He has early onset Alzheimer's, and he's probably not going to live much longer."

"I'm so sorry. That's really hard. Are you close with him?"

He stared blankly, his eyes no more focused than the clouds. "I don't really want to talk about it."

"I totally understand." She cleared her throat and put on what she hoped was a nonthreatening smile. "So Nathan has me taking over for you. I was hoping you could show me a little bit about my job."

"I can do that." Without another word, Bryan brushed by her. He moved so quickly down the hall on his long legs, Winter had to jog to keep up. When he came into his former office, he sat at the computer, turned it on, and started fiddling with it.

Winter had to fetch her chair from Melissa's office to sit down next to him.

"Nathan's appointment book is probably the most important thing." Bryan opened the calendar app on the screen. "He never has any fucking clue what's going on, so you have to remind him. Like a child."

Winter pulled a mute, close-lipped smile and blinked. "All righty, then."

Bryan took a slow, deep breath. Then he dropped his hand from the mouse. "I can smell your shampoo."

"Oh, yeah?" As if she weren't on high alert already, every hair on her body stood up. "It's supposed to be jasmine, I think."

"Smells more like tuberose." He inhaled deeply through his nose again.

If Nathan had said such a thing, she would've been afflicted by the powerful urge to start breaking his bones. But there was something just awkward enough about Bryan that she wasn't sure if he was coming on to her, or if he just really liked smelling things.

He still hadn't looked at her, not really.

"Do you know a lot about flowers?" she asked.

"I like to be outside."

"You're a climber, right? Like everybody else around here."

"Not like everybody else. Climbing is a business to them. For me, it's my passion. It's my life."

"I bet you know all the best climbing spots around here."

"Of course I do."

"I was in El Barranco State Park last weekend. It's pretty flat, though." She giggled at herself to keep the mood light. "I had a hard time finding anything to climb."

"There's a crack in the west, following a tributary."

"Like a ravine?"

His eyes flashed to hers, sharp as needles. Wherever his attention had gone when she walked in, it was here now. "Exactly. There's some good cave climbing around there, too, if you don't mind the dark."

"Do you mind it?"

"I hate the dark."

"Does that mean you don't go cave climbing?"

"I go all the time. I'm very good at learning to live with things that I hate."

As his eyes shot in the direction of Lynch's office, his words struck chords deep in Winter's gut. This time, she had to put her hands up. "Why learn to live with it if there's something you can do to avoid it or even change it?"

Bryan turned toward her and searched her face before returning his attention to his computer.

Winter thought the conversation was going pretty well, considering. She could dig in deeper. "Did you and Christina used to climb together?"

Bryan visibly tensed. She watched his Adam's apple as he swallowed a lump.

"I'm sorry. If you don't want to talk about it, just say that, and I will never bring it up again. I just know when I've lost people close to me, sometimes it helps to talk about them. And it can be nice when somebody asks."

He met her eyes again, softer now. "I met Christina because of climbing."

"At Cumberland, right?"

"No. I worked with her and Aliyah Andry at a climbing gym before we came here."

"I didn't know that. So how long had you known each other?" The less Winter pretended to know, the better.

"Two years." He sat back from the keyboard and folded his hands in his lap. "Christina and me went way back."

"And Aliyah?"

His lips twitched. "Yeah. I knew her for a while too."

Winter marked the use of the past tense. Aliyah hadn't yet been found, which meant she wasn't officially gone. But she decided now was not the best time to address that. The conversation felt very delicate, like trying to keep a flame alive in the rain. One false word and she might smother the whole thing. "Can you make any sense of what's been going on around here?"

"You mean, the murders?"

"What do you think's happening? Why would anybody want to hurt Tucker or Helen?"

Bryan looked up at her again and, this time, held her gaze.

She tried to keep her face open, innocent, and curious. Not a private investigator undercover at all.

"I never knew how blue *blue* could be."

She wrinkled her nose. "What?"

"Your eyes…"

A hard knock at the door startled them both. Lynch poked his horse's ass in. "Yo, Bry. Get sweet Sam here into to the HR database for me. Give her full access."

"What? Why?"

"'Cause I said so, Bryan. Dammit!" He wasn't angry, just a typical alpha male strutting around and pounding his chest.

"Seems like he just wants us to work as a team on both jobs." She forced a laugh to calm her nerves and shrugged. "So, actually, I'm kind of your assistant, huh?"

Her words landed on him slowly, each one plainly registering on his face. But she wasn't sure what any of the little twitches meant.

"I'd better get on that." Bryan cast his gaze down and, in a second, was out the door, leaving her alone to stare after him.

37

For the rest of the day, Bryan didn't say two words to Winter, other than to make excuses why she couldn't have the HR files yet. There could be a lot of reasons why—nervous with all the death surrounding him, scared Nathan hired her to replace him, genuinely unfamiliar with the HR computer system, as he claimed. Or he could be the company serial killer.

Winter knew better than to leap to conclusions without evidence, but that didn't stop her mind from circling back time and time again.

She left Cumberland after six o'clock and headed back to her office. Her whole body was twisted in knots, her brain ruminating and storming all at once.

Only years of experience had allowed her to focus on her work today. But the moment she exited Cumberland and came out of undercover mode, thoughts of last night's events washed over her.

First day back from leave, and Noah had shot somebody. Not that she blamed him or thought it could in any way be avoided. Noah was not reckless. He was damn good at what he did, and whatever force he thought was necessary, she supported one hundred percent. But unless Weston Falkner felt exactly the same way, this had the potential to become a big problem.

There was a part of her that wanted to march down to that man's office and scold him for being too stupid to realize how amazing Noah was. Her husband had told her very nicely, but firmly, not to do that.

Carl Gardner had been pronounced DOA at the hospital. On the positive side, now his whole setup had been confiscated by the Bureau for a full digital forensic examination. Gardner had managed to put bullets in two of the computers. But unless he miraculously hit the hard drive, that wouldn't deter the investigation.

Winter stepped into the offices of Black Investigations to find it empty. She breathed a sigh of relief. Yet another situation that squeezed at her intestines. All she wanted was a moment to herself. No cameras. No men leering at her. No ridiculously enthusiastic assistants. Just herself, her coffee, and the triple chocolate muffins she picked up on the way over.

Winter closed the blinds in her office. She picked some ambient music and pressed play. One hour, that was all she needed. One hour to clear her head so she could see the truth.

The first notes played, but before the melody could even pick up, the door popped open, and Ariel bubbled inside.

"Dammit." Winter's back drooped in disappointment.

"Winter!" Ariel rushed closer. Her tablet was curled under one arm, and in the other was a bag from their favorite lunch spot. "I'm so glad you're here."

"This is why mountain climbing is better. Nobody can get to you."

"What?"

"Nothing." With a sigh, she hit pause on the music.

"I brought food. I have so much I need to talk to you about."

Winter looked at the bag, which she knew contained buttery submarine sandwiches and freshly fried chips. She looked at Ariel, who was biting her lips like she might explode.

Winter took the bag. "Your peace offering of food is accepted. You may speak."

"Thank you." She hurried closer and sat down. "Okay, so. Tucker Hicks—"

"He's gone. I'll tell you who I want to know more about." Winter bit into the decadent hoagie. "Bryan Green."

"Oh, well, Bryan and Christina were both kind of offline, but Aliyah Andry posted all the time. Six months ago, she posted a picture of Bryan and Christina and said, 'My two besties are finally dating! Hashtag cutest couple ever.'"

"Can I see the picture?"

"Yeah." Ariel passed over her tablet. "Anyway, I already started looking into Bryan. And I found some stuff."

Winter examined the photo. Somewhere in the woods, Bryan stood with his arm over Christina's shoulder. She looked so happy. And he was smiling too.

"So his dad is an epic piece of work." Unburdened of her tablet, Ariel fiddled with the chunky beads of turquoise on her bracelet. "He has a long criminal record. Domestic abuse, DUI, breaking and entering, assault with a deadly weapon, robbery."

"That's a sheet."

"There's more. He's done multiple stints in prison. The last time he was in for vehicular assault. And get this. Bryan's mother killed herself."

"His mother and then his girlfriend…?" Winter's mind

flashed back to Bryan, clouds in his eyes as he gazed out of the window at nothing. "That poor man."

"I think he's the killer." Ariel was bouncing on the balls of her feet, she was so excited. "Crazy abusive dad. Dead mom. Horrible childhood. He must be so traumatized."

The buttery bread turned sour on Winter's tongue. "Being traumatized doesn't necessarily make a person a killer."

Ariel's eyes widened like a shot. "That's not what I meant. I wasn't talking about you…"

"Of course not." She let it drop because there wasn't a thing either of them could say to change it. "So where is Bryan's dad these days?"

"He has early onset Alzheimer's and lives in a memory care facility."

The more she thought about it, Winter realized she needed to talk to someone who knew Bryan well. Get a feeling for his character. But that list of people seemed to be getting shorter all the time. The best she could manage was Nathan Lynch, his boss.

Putting down her hoagie, Winter picked up the phone and called him. He didn't answer the first time. Or the second. On the final ring of her third attempt, he finally picked up.

"What?" The clickety-clack of an engine reached her ear, something winding down, and a crunch like broken plastic. She might not have thought much of it, except this was the landline in his office.

"Hi, Nathan," Winter said. *A paper shredder, maybe.* "Whatcha doin'?

"Working."

"What's that noise?"

"Nothing. Construction. What do you want? I'm busy."

"I just wanted to tell you I have a strong lead. You might not see me for a little bit 'cause I've gotta follow this down."

"Sure. Whatever."

"Okay. Talk to you later."

"Wait. Who's the lead?"

On that note, Winter hung up, fully intending to deny ever having heard the question. Might as well let the man think she was busy, give him a silent green light to carry on destroying evidence. Meanwhile, she could get the drop on him and catch him in the act.

She texted Noah. *Meet me at Cumberland in thirty minutes.*

38

Winter used her fob to get into the locked offices of Cumberland. The overhead lights were off, but water still whooshed from the waterfall wall in the huge atrium, overwhelming any other ambient noise.

With Noah following close behind, she made her way through the showroom and to the offices. More closed doors and dim lights. More darkness. But Nathan Lynch's door at the end of the hall was ajar.

A warning tore through Winter like red lightning spiking from the carpet. She drew her gun. "He always closes his door."

Noah nodded and drew his weapon as well. Gingerly, they approached the door—Winter up front, Noah in back. She pushed it open with her foot and peered inside.

A huge rectangular shredder was front and center, along with three black garbage bags overflowing with shredded documents. Open file boxes littered the room. The wall safe, which she already knew about, hung open and empty.

They checked the blind spots of the room and found

nothing, so Winter holstered her gun and took out her phone to make a recording of the space.

Sitting on Lynch's desk was a monitor hooked up to a small black box about the size of an external disk drive. On closer inspection, Winter realized the box was a DVD player and the screen was on, the DVD logo bouncing off the sides. Winter opened a file box next to the player and found a stack of jewel cases containing DVD-ROMs. They looked like home movies.

Winter plucked the first and read the handwritten title out loud. "Aliyah from Behind: Screamer." She perused the others. Melissa. Helen. Some names she'd never heard of.

Oh, Helen... She hadn't told Winter that she was a victim too.

Bile rose in her throat. Had Nathan set this up? Maybe he was so sad to have to destroy these things that he'd wanted to watch each of them one last time. It would explain why he hadn't destroyed them yet.

Pulling another box closer, Winter opened the lid. Printed photographs. Winter yanked out a handful. As she began flicking through them, she realized the true depth of Nathan Lynch's voyeurism. Pictures of every woman who worked at Cumberland. Walking down the hall, having lunch, sitting on the toilet. Using the company gym, getting undressed in the locker rooms. Naked in the showers.

Melissa, Helen, Aliyah...Sam Drewitt on day one in his office. They were all there.

Noah stepped up behind her. "Is this all what I think it is?"

She pressed her hand to her stomach, sick to her core. "Everything we need to nail Nathan Lynch to the wall."

"Yeah." Noah's gaze darted over the evidence. "So where the hell is the bastard?" He looked through the titles on the DVDs. "Never been so happy to see you not make the cut," he joked.

"What did you just say?"

"I said—"

"You said I didn't make the cut." Winter went back to the box of DVDs and looked at every title. Then she picked up the box of photos and studied every face. "You know who else didn't make the cut?"

"Who?"

"Christina. Follow me."

She headed to the computer in Bryan's office—to which she'd been given all the passwords—and was able to log into the security camera feed. She rolled back to five o'clock.

On the grainy screen, she watched everybody start heading home. At six, she left in her Honda.

Bryan Green left at six fifteen in a dark-blue Hyundai. She also kept an eye on Nathan's Tesla, parked, as always, near its own little charging station. She'd called him and spoken to him in his office right about seven. He was still there, in the building. Alone.

"What are you thinking?"

"Look."

At fourteen minutes after seven, a white Jeep Wrangler that Winter had never seen before pulled into the lot. It had a set of high-end, off-roading tires that could scale a building. It parked diagonally across three spaces. Bryan Green, dressed exactly as he had been an hour before, got out of the vehicle and went inside.

Sixteen minutes later, at seven thirty on the nose, he came back out and got into his Jeep. It looked like he might drive away. Instead, he pulled around the building and backed up to one of the loading docks.

Winter tried to switch cameras to catch the view back there, but the feed had been disabled during the time Bryan was inside.

"I think there are no photos or videos of Christina here because—"

"Nathan Lynch never made any," Noah finished. "But why?"

She remembered the lost look Nathan had on his face that day in the hall. *You remind me of...* "Because he was in love with Christina."

Noah inhaled sharply. "That means this whole killing spree is about her, and it also means that—"

"Bryan has Nathan," Winter breathed.

"Which means he might already be dead."

Winter pushed away from the desk. "Come on. Let's go find the worthless son of a bitch."

39

Nathan's wrists and arms were lashed together behind his back, wrapped in so much rope, plaited with knots. He hadn't quite gone numb, unfortunately. His arms felt like they were being slowly ripped from their sockets.

His legs were in a similar state, wrapped up like a caterpillar in its cocoon. Knots dug in behind his knees. Dozens of hard, sharp little knots were tied all around his genitals, pressing into his dick, encircling his nuts like they'd been wrapped in barbed wire. The rope must've been looped between his legs before it was wound around him.

He lay on his side in the back of Bryan's Jeep, moaning as every curve and every bounce drove the knots in deeper. A knot had been shoved in his mouth, choking him. Pain arced through every inch of his body.

Bryan was behind the wheel, racing down the road. He was talking to someone, not Nathan. And nobody else was there.

This was what happened to Parker and Aliyah and Helen and Tucker. Strangled to death in the back of this Jeep or thrown over a cliff to break upon the rocks at the bottom. What about Melissa? Had he caught her too?

He's going to kill you, Nate.

Nathan often talked to himself in the third person in tense situations—so he wouldn't get distracted by emotions, including fear. *But you can't let that happen. You can't be murdered by Bryan fucking Green! You have to get out of this.*

Bryan wasn't the only one who played with ropes. Back in college, Nathan had made a habit of tying people up—tight and serious with real knots and real technique—then leaving them in strange places. He only did it to people who got way too drunk and passed out on the floor of the frat house. Sometimes, girls who'd passed out in his bed. It was funny. And he was a mountain climber. He had a lot of rope.

When his frat brothers finally ganged up on him, Nathan had untied himself from all their elaborate knots in less than five minutes. But unlike his college buddies, Bryan knew what he was doing.

Everything hurt and moving made it worse, but Nathan kept fighting, wiggling and weaving, looking for weaknesses in the binds.

"I see you back there," Bryan growled. "I bet you have something you'd like to say right now, don't you?"

Nathan screamed against the rough gag filling his mouth.

"I know that feeling. Like someone isn't listening to you. Like when they tell you to stop, but you don't stop." He slammed on the brakes. Nathan's untethered body crashed hard into the seat backs. The knots were all driving into him at once, like being body-slammed naked onto gravel.

"You're going to stop this time, Nathan." Bryan eased back onto the road. "I can see why somebody like Tucker would admire you. You're the King Midas of whores, right? All it takes is one touch from you, and a good woman is ruined forever. Yet they line up to have it done to them over and over. I don't understand it."

Nathan tried to yell, but all that did was cut off his air supply. The gag filled up so much of his throat, it was even a struggle to draw breath through his nostrils.

"You take advantage of them in every way. Seeing you work is like watching the devil. The way you charm them, lie to them, make them feel like they're the only woman in your universe, take whatever you want whenever you want, make them think it was all their idea, trap them with money, physically dominate them. You teach them how to be good little sluts and then take them or leave them at your leisure. Let your underlings clean up the leftovers."

In the impact, Nathan's arm had shifted just enough to give a little slack on his left wrist.

"Most woman are too weak to fight you. And any woman who won't fight to the death to keep her purity deserves whatever she gets. As do men like Parker and Tucker," he spat out their names, "who would stand back and watch, or even help you hide your filth from everyone."

One hand wiggled free. Not the wrist or the arm, but at least the fingers. If he could get under the lashing…

"I called your wife, Nathan."

Everything stopped cold, Nathan's mind screeching to a halt.

"She's used to me calling, usually to tell her you're going to be late. Again. This time, I asked her to come down to Cumberland. She has a key, of course. I told her to just come in and head straight to your office. And in there, I left out your DVD player and all your disks. I told her to make herself comfortable and watch a movie."

His wife had always said if she ever caught him cheating, she'd divorce him, taking with her the kids and all her money—ninety percent of their combined net worth. Though he grew up very wealthy, Nathan's father had cut him off just after college, telling him he needed to make his own way in the world. Nathan only still talked to the old man in the hopes of getting that money back.

Charlotte was his seed money, his nest egg, his starting point. He couldn't lose her.

"Don't worry about the money, Nathan. I'm going to kill you tonight. It doesn't matter. Wrap the spool with the tag end. Overhand, use the standing. Not a such a bad way to die. Second knot to the tag. Pull the standing tight. First to second on the spool. Drive the knots to the bottom."

This guy is fucking nuts. No wonder she broke up with him. C'mon, Nate buddy, think.

Nathan thrashed his head back and forth. *Get this thing off me!*

But the only sound that got past the ropes were muffled groans.

Bryan slammed on the brakes again, this time swerving off to the side of the road. He put the Jeep in park, leaving the engine running.

In a flash, he had the hatch open and was above Nathan with the knife. He slashed Nathan's cheek, cutting rope and skin. With a snarl, Bryan ripped the gag out of his mouth.

Nathan gasped, coughed, and hissed in pain as blood dripped down his chin. "Bryan! What the fuck is wrong with you?"

"You have something to say?" He snatched a fistful of his hair in one hand and punched him in the face with the other.

The first strike broke Nathan's nose. He spluttered, trying to form words. But Bryan hit him again and again and again.

"Shut up! You worthless piece of shit. Don't you fucking look at me! I'll cut you while you're sleeping. You killed her. You killed her! You killed my Christina!"

After what seemed like an eternity, Bryan finally pulled back his fists.

Nathan's blood had spattered the interior and the windows, his mouth and eyes already beginning to swell. Like bee stings, the pain in the knot welts intensified.

Nathan spat out a mouthful of blood. "I never hurt her. I never killed her. What are you talking about?"

"You're a liar!" Bryan snatched one of the ropes on Nathan's chest and twisted. Knots dug in harder, scoring his flesh.

"Please! Stop! I never hurt Christina. Please…"

"I already know the truth. I know what you did to her."

"I didn't!"

"Why keep lying?" Bryan twisted the rope even tighter.

"I'm not lying! I swear!"

Bryan eased off the rope just half a twist. "Go on, Nathan. Tell your last lie. See if it'll save you this time."

Nathan's eyes fell closed as he fought for each breath. In his mind, he saw Christina. Beautiful girl with a brilliant smile. So bright and eager to learn, with a degree in business that proved she could be taught. Nathan thought he really could make something of her.

The more time he spent with Christina, the more he liked her. She was different from the other girls. Sweet, sensitive, sincere. Everything he wasn't. Nathan usually ate girls like Christina for breakfast, but there was something different about her. She was haunted by something, keeping secrets, dodging questions. The mystery was almost as engaging as the rest of her.

He found himself beginning to care about her. He'd think about her when she wasn't around. Worry how she was doing. How she was feeling.

Sure, he flirted with her relentlessly, but he never made

an advance, not once. Until the day she flirted back. The chemistry between them was steamy. A hint of urgency in her eyes and in her voice. And she was reaching toward Nathan to rescue her from her own galumphing boyfriend.

Nathan had never thought of Bryan as dangerous, just mediocre. *"The only reason a girl like you goes with a guy like that is if she's lacking self-confidence."* He used to tell her that. Then he would hold her tight and kiss her passionately. She would play coy, and the blush that colored her pale cheeks was prettier than any sunrise he'd ever seen.

Nathan started crying, and not from the pain. "I never hurt Christina. I loved her. I loved her so much."

"No!" Bryan screamed. His eyes darted this way and that like a caged animal. He snatched Nathan by his feet and dragged him out onto the roadway.

He plopped hard onto the stinging gravel and moaned in pain.

They were somewhere out in the wilderness, just pulled over to the side of the road. The Jeep was somewhat hidden by some thick, low-hanging leaves.

"What are you doing?" Nathan twisted under the knots. "You have to let me go. They're going to catch you. If you let me go, I could help you. Money for a good lawyer."

Holding on to a rope attached to Nathan's feet, Bryan dragged him onto the road and laid him out on his stomach, perpendicular to the Jeep. He wedged his feet under the back wheel like chocks under a plane. If Bryan threw the car in reverse, both of Nathan's feet would be crushed.

"What the hell are you doing?" Nathan struggled to pull his feet back. Maybe it was the friction of the knot against the tire or his odd position, he wasn't sure what, but he couldn't get them to move.

Bryan stood and got back into the driver's seat.

"No! Please! You can't!" Nathan yanked at his bound feet, his eyes darting. Only then did he see the static line tied to the axle.

The engine flared, and the wheel slumped into gear.

"Bryan! No! Please, God, no!"

But only the trees and the dark night sky heard his cries.

40

En route to El Barranco State Park, with Noah behind the wheel of his F-350 as big, fat raindrops struck the windshield, Winter called Deputy Mullaney to update him.

"Primary suspect is Bryan Green. Caucasian, thirty years old, six-two, brown hair, driving a white Jeep Wrangler." She gave him the license plate number. "We believe he has a victim. Nathan Lynch. Caucasian, forty-three, six-one."

"You think he's headed to the same dumping grounds?"

"Not exactly but close. He's familiar enough with the area to use lesser-known roads. Fire access roads, ATV trails, places the general public don't go."

"There are more of those places than people realize, Ms. Black."

"Whatever it takes. You need to get all your people out. Air support, drones. Whatever you have. This guy's killed at least three people, and he's going to kill again."

"Yes, ma'am. I'll send out everything we've got." Before he hung up, Mullaney asked the question that had been on Winter's mind. "Why did Green do all this?"

She knew the answer, or at least part of it. It'd been

written in that twitch in his lip when she asked him about Aliyah. In the hatred that dripped from his voice when he spoke of Lynch. In his sad eyes the first time she'd bumped into him in the hall, when he'd warned her about what might happen.

The only person at Cumberland who'd really warned her.

"This is all about his girlfriend who died by suicide about three weeks ago, Christina Norris."

That hung in the air between them for a moment.

"You know what, Lyle, let's meet above the ravine."

"By the first body? Where we found the red and orange tape on the trees?"

"Yes. Something tells me that's where it all began and ended for Bryan and Christina."

41

Nathan Lynch faded in and out of consciousness, shock and blood loss overwhelming him. Both his ankles were shattered as Bryan drove over them, back and forth, before snatching him up and throwing him back into the Jeep. Nathan left his blood all over the roadway. Now he was shivering, fighting for every breath, and losing his grip on reality. Some part of him hoped this was just the world's worst nightmare.

Bryan had brought him to this place in the wilderness to kill him. And there was nothing Nathan could do to stop it. He couldn't even scream. Who would hear him? He trembled and hoped death would come quickly.

When he came to, he was lashed to a tree, his worthless feet dangling under him, radiating pain. Bryan was mumbling to himself while stringing him up, going over the steps on how to tie various knots as if instructing a newbie.

"Tie a half hitch with the tag end itself." Bryan followed his own instructions, sometimes slowly and methodically, other times at double or triple speed. "The mainline just happens to be through it. So the mainline's not included in the half hitch, per se."

"Bryan…" Nathan's voice choked on a blood clot wedged in his throat. He spat it out. "Bryan, you don't have to do this."

"Tie another half hitch to the very end of the line."

"I've learned my lesson. Please." Every moment that he was conscious, Nathan wriggled against the line. But the hope of escaping Bryan's expert web had grown slim. The only other option was to beg, so as hot tears streamed down his cheeks, that was what he did. "Please, Bryan, forgive me. I never hurt her."

"You never learn your lesson!" Bryan snapped, spittle flying from his lips. He punched Nathan in the face with all his might. "That's the problem with you. You worthless little shithead! You're just like your mother!"

Nathan twisted and sobbed, gasping through blood. "What the fuck are you talking about?"

Taking a step back, Bryan set his hands on his hips and admired his work like a crafter. "People like you never learn. They lock you up, take away everything, but they don't stop."

"Who the fuck are you talking to? Bryan, please, listen. I'm not the world's most stand-up guy. Is that what you want? Fine, I admit it. But I loved Christina with all my heart. I was in love with her."

"Shut the fuck up. I know you were, you snake. I saw you. I saw you through the hole! You can't leave even one woman for the rest of us. You gotta have them all, you selfish prick!"

That was when it hit Nathan. Christina must've broken up with Bryan like she said she would. To start fresh. Which meant…

"Bryan." Nathan choked out his name, openly sobbing, tears mixed with blood dripping off his battered face. "Did you…" He couldn't get out the words. The answer terrified him, but he had to know. "Did you kill Christina?"

"It's your fault. You did! You made her kill herself."

"No…oh, no, Bryan, no." Nathan coughed up blood, strangled by emotions that had been foreign to him up 'til this very moment. "But she was so beautiful, so perfect. Why? Why…"

"It was the only way to escape you!"

Nathan knew her suicide had felt wrong. She was different and sweet but not…she wasn't that kind of fragile… to hang herself by a noose. Snatching a flash of anger by the reins, Nathan spat a mouthful of blood at Bryan. It speckled his shirt and the rope in his hands. "You killed her! You fucking maniac, you dumb fucking dope! You killed her…"

"No, I didn't. She loved me." His face was flat, like it always was. Like everything about Bryan—just flat and boring. "She loved me, not you!"

Nathan had thought that, too, until the first night Christina stayed late to talk to him about problems she was having at work. Problems with Bryan.

As Nathan literally hung onto life, laughter—crazy and hopeless—rippled through him, trumping the pain. *Why not laugh when your life is over, Nate buddy? Why not...*

And when your life is over, why not tell the truth?

"Christina came on to me." An electric thrill shot up Nathan's spine. Or maybe it was death calling, short-circuiting his system.

Bryan snarled like a wildcat watching prey. "You're lying. You seduced her."

"She came to my office after hours to complain about you." Nathan coughed up more blood. "She said you scared her. I offered to fire you, and she hugged me. Isn't that sweet?"

"Stop!"

"You know it's true. You spied on me through some hole, like you just said. You're no better than me." Nathan's lips curled into a bloody smile. "Except I got the girl."

Bryan's arm flew back and smashed Nathan across the face so hard, he thought his neck would snap.

Nathan closed his eyes tight and braced for the next blow, hoping this would be the one to knock him out and end his pain.

But it didn't come. Something else had arrested Bryan's attention.

A bullhorn in the distance.

In his haze, Nathan could barely make out the shouting, but he knew a cop when he heard one.

They'd come for him.

"Help!" Nathan screamed, but Bryan was on him before he could make another sound. A flash of silver caught in the moonlight. And then sharpness shot through Nathan's side.

Only when Bryan pulled out the knife and held it up near his face did Nathan realize what had happened. He drew back to plunge the knife in again when a second blast from the bullhorn sounded, much closer than before.

Bryan clenched the knife tight and raced away into the forest.

42

Winter and Noah reached the trailhead and parked on the gravel next to Deputy Mullaney's giant white truck. He was there with several other state park deputies in full gear. Winter hopped out of the truck before Noah even had it in park.

"We haven't been able to locate his vehicle yet." Mullaney stepped up close to Winter, a bullhorn in his grip. "We've cleared the area of visitors, though there weren't many on the trails this late. APD and FBI are on the way. Choppers too."

"This place is like a second home to Bryan. He'd know all the back ways and secret paths." She walked closer to the edge of the ravine and snatched up one of the harnesses waiting there. "We'll have better luck on foot."

By the time Noah came over, Winter had herself strapped up and tied into the line with the classic figure-eight knot.

"I sent a few cars the long way around to drive down into the ravine." Mullaney stepped into his own harness. "They should be there soon."

"Have you gotten any word on Melissa?" She stepped up with her heels to the ledge, readying herself to sit back.

"Yes, ma'am. She finally answered her phone." The corner of his mouth curved up. "She's in Majorca."

Winter sighed with relief. "So she's safe?"

"Safe as can be. I guess she finally had enough of all the bull crud at Cumberland and decided to quit without notice to stick it in Nathan's craw."

"Or she didn't want to get tortured and killed, so she slipped away in the night." Melissa was a survivor, no one's victim. Winter hoped she'd be okay moving forward. "Aliyah?"

Mullaney shook his head. "Search and Rescue's been at it for almost a week now. Not to mention dozens of community members and her family. She's pretty popular. It's not impossible she's out there, but it is unlikely."

A high-pitched shriek cut off Winter's response.

Mullaney set a finger to the trigger on the bullhorn. "Bryan Green. This is Deputy Mullaney with the El Barranco State Park Rangers…"

He paused as a muffled scream sounded from down among the moonlight-soaked trees. A man's voice. Then another strangled plea.

Winter didn't hesitate. She sat back into gravity and pushed off the side of the cliff, rappelling down as quickly as possible. Noah yelled her name from above, still calling out to her as her boots hit the ground. For the first time, she didn't wobble. She clicked off the carabiner and took off into the woods in the vague direction of the scream.

Her gun was in her hand, her heart in her throat. Winter moved swiftly through the brush since she was wearing proper clothes this time, nothing biting at her thighs or scratching her ankles.

She hopped over the boulders where she'd found the

blood-soaked ropes Bryan used to restrain Aliyah Andry and headed straight down the ravine parallel to the cliff. She bent back a sapling and scrambled over a heavy moss overhang. A rock the size of Beulah with a tall, jagged crest blocked her way. It was surrounded by what looked like blackberry bushes on either side—thorny gray brambles in the moonlight.

"Help me! Please!" The voice was faint but close.

She holstered her weapon and threw herself at the rock, slick with moisture from the spattering of rain that had fallen while they were driving up. She lost her grip and slipped back a few inches before managing to drag herself over the sharp edge to survey the open ravine.

A man was strapped to a tree with so much rope, he looked like a mummy. His head was bound, too, wrapped to the trunk like the hilt of a Japanese sword.

Winter hopped down. She put two fingers to her lips and whistled loudly to lead the others. Then she drew her weapon and approached.

"Nathan?"

There wasn't much, but every inch of his exposed skin glowed shock-white in the moonlight. Something wet poured from his side like black tar. Blood.

The sound of footfalls and shouts came from behind her, Noah's voice a harsh boom against the silence. "Winter!"

"I'm here!" she called over one shoulder, then turned back to Nathan. Taking out her pocketknife, she carefully cut the rope from his neck.

He gasped in some air.

"Bryan..." He wheezed and spat up blood that trickled down his chin. "He's the killer."

"Which way did he go?"

"I don't know! He just disappeared. Sam, um, Winter,"

Nathan moaned in pain, "he killed Christina. He...killed her." He let out a small cry of agony and passed out.

"Nathan, stay with me!"

At last, Mullaney, Noah, and two other deputies caught up.

"Winter!" Noah dashed to her side.

Mullaney and the others hurried to assist Nathan, two knives working at once to cut him loose. When the ropes around his forehead broke free, he lurched forward and vomited pink sludge onto the front of his shirt and in the face of the cop who was bracing him up while the others cut.

Mullaney got on his radio and called for an emergency medical helicopter.

"Medevac is on their way too." Mullaney looked directly at Winter. "Ten minutes."

Every hand was on Nathan. As they lowered him to the ground, a foot touched the earth, and he screamed in agony. In the darkness, Winter couldn't tell exactly what was wrong with his feet, other than they were flopping and looked like the wrong shape.

She peered closer. They'd been crushed, the bones shattered. What the hell had Bryan done to him? "His feet are broken!"

They lifted his legs to lay him on his back. The rangers tended to the wound in his side after that.

Winter forced herself to breathe through her nose, trying to listen for noises beyond the commotion of Nathan's weeping and the pounding of her own heart.

She'd taken a few steps toward the edge of the forest when a flare of pain struck her frontal lobe like being hit with a baseball.

Her hand went to her temple, and she leaned over her knees. She smelled blood before she felt it on her upper lip. A headache, that was all this was. And the nosebleed that often accompanied them. A shock of lightning to her brain. She blinked through the pain and glanced up.

A flicker of faint, shimmering red light danced through the trees, as if it were fleeing through the shadows.

Her gift was showing her the way.

"That way!" Winter pointed but didn't wait for a response from the others before she took off running into the woods.

The red glow didn't last forever, sometimes only for a few seconds, before evaporating back into the atmosphere. There was no time to waste.

43

They'd found me. I could only hope I'd inflicted enough damage on Nathan that he would die before they could save him.

I tied into the rope I'd left hanging from the lip of the cave and swung down into the darkness.

I hit the slick wall, lost balance, and slammed against the side.

Dammit!

My knife clattered down into the abyss.

Focus, just focus. And breathe.

I couldn't think about my knife now. I had other ways of defending myself anyway. I had to get down to my hiding spot. They might find my Jeep, and if they did, my life as Bryan Green—mild-mannered nobody, everybody's whipping boy—was over.

I didn't really care. If I could wait them out, I could sneak out of the park. I had a stash of cash in my hiding place, and it was at least enough to catch a Greyhound out of Austin and get up to Dallas. To Sunny Stones Assisted Living and Memory Care, where dear ole dad was waiting.

Once he was dead, then it didn't really matter what happened to me. I could leave the country, disappear. The nightmare would finally be over.

I flicked on my headlamp, dodging deeper into the darkness. Most people didn't know about this cave, not even the rangers. It was well hidden by brush at the very edge of the ravine. I hadn't been down here since killing Parker, but it had been one of our spots.

Water dripped over the edges, slicking the already-smooth rocks. I wished I could've gotten down it without a rope, but after the first several meters of wriggling through like a lizard, there came a long open drop. The only way down was with rope. More importantly, that was also the only way back up.

They'd never find my line. I'd hidden it too well, especially in this darkness. The search parties had been going over this place for days, and the line was right as I'd left it. My plan B.

The sound of helicopters whirred overhead, little more than a hum in the gathering silence of the cave. I heard the echo of far-off voices. Was that Nathan screaming in pain? God, I hoped so. Unbearable pain was the next best thing to death for him.

Now I hoped they'd save him, so surgeons could try to sew him back up, attempt to fix those pancake feet. I hoped it was all very painful and unsuccessful, that he'd never be able to climb again. They'd call his wife, and she'd go to the hospital, her head full of all the things I'd told her in my message. Things she might've seen at his office if she went there. She'd sit in the waiting room, waiting for her terrible husband to survive surgery so she could nail his ass to the wall.

And someday, when her children were older, she could

tell them the truth about what a useless, evil hunk of human shit their father was.

Then I heard it—a shuffle and a scuffle at the entrance of my cave. And I felt a tug on the rope still hooked to me.

The blood drained from my face. They'd found me.

But that was impossible!

Now I didn't have any other option. Whoever it was—even just some innocent cop doing their job—I had to take them out. They'd left me no choice. This was bigger than me, and I had to get to Dallas.

They tugged on my rope again, harder this time. But there were no voices filtering down to me. No whistles, no bullhorns, no shouting. Maybe this cop was all alone.

Perfect.

I let out some slack and hopped down into the cavern.

To the far left, a cranny led down farther into the system, eventually dropping off into an underground lake. But here, there was steady footing. Stalactites above, the gentle drip of water. I estimated the cavern at about two hundred square feet with a high enough roof that I could stand up straight.

That was where I would leave their body.

I unhooked my line, letting whoever was after me pull it up. Would they tie in and try to climb down?

With a deep breath to steady myself, I clicked off my headlamp and was immediately plunged into total darkness. Then I pulled a short length of securing line from my belt and wrapped it once over my right hand. I pressed myself to the edge to wait for them, silent and still. When they were an inch off, their body practically pressed against mine, I would choke them out.

If more came, I'd kill them, too, then make my way out of here on foot.

A shower of small rocks and dust brushed my shoulder. They were coming. It wasn't long before I recognized the faint, intermittent glow of someone else's flashlight drawing closer. They grunted, a woman's voice echoing through the cave and landing on my ears.

The rope creaked as I wrapped it tighter around my hand.

Just a little closer now.

Like all the rest, she would never see me coming.

44

Winter never would've found the cave without the red glow. It would also be her guide once she went inside. But if she hesitated, she might lose it.

She wasn't entirely sure what she might find down there. Bryan Green could've fled to this place. Or it could be Aliyah Andry down there, cold and alone. Dead, maybe. But she was led here, and she had to go in.

The thrum of Winter's heart in her ears was like the rush of a waterfall. The run, the climb, the adrenaline. Her body was primed and bursting with energy, like a transformer about to explode.

Part of her mind was still wrapped up with Nathan on that tree. He was an odious person who deserved to be punished for all the things he'd done, but the horror of his condition was unshakable. Especially when she thought of Helen, Aliyah, Parker Roy, and even Tucker Hicks, enduring the same agonies.

She stared at the nondescript hole in the ground camouflaged in thick foliage. But the red glow led her right to a boulder, and that was when she saw it. Red and orange tape, faded, stuck to a rock a foot above her eyeline. The same tape that was by Parker Roy's body.

She kicked around the foliage at her feet and spotted a line of bright-green nylon climbing rope. It was secured well and fell into the blackness.

Green had said that he hated the dark but was very good at learning to live with things he hated.

He was down there. She could feel it in her blood. Emotions were at Winter's peak, heightening her senses and sharpening her resolve.

She'd never gone spelunking before and wasn't overly excited to start now. Before lowering herself gingerly into the darkness, her feet against the slick wall, she clicked on the flashlight attached to the top pocket of her windbreaker.

Winter put a hand to her mouth to call out to him, but a sharp shock to her frontal lobe stopped her. Like the legs of a spider, a chill crawled down her back. He was down there. She knew it as well as she knew her own name, and she could sense him concealing himself in the dark.

She had no idea how far into the cave he'd gone. But Bryan Green knew this place like a second home.

Winter glanced back over her shoulder, wondering if she should wait for the others. But what if there was another way out? What if this had been his emergency escape plan all along?

The best chance of catching him was to go in.

Before Winter could think about it too much longer, she dropped over the ledge and lowered herself down. Her fingers, already growing small callouses from what little climbing she'd done in the past week, gripped the rope. Rubber soles held her steady.

The opening of the cave was incredibly narrow, and in some places, the easiest way to go down was to press her back against the adjacent wall and walk with her feet. Just like she'd done at Cumberland when she'd taken the flag from the Summit.

Winter sucked on her bottom lip to keep her breath quiet and focus her attention. She had no idea what was under her. Other than a serial killer, of course. She couldn't trust that anything would catch her if she fell. Once again, she had to put all her faith into her own hands, her own muscles, her own mind.

The slow, steady drip of water was interrupted by a clunk in the darkness below. Perhaps Bryan shifting his weight. Or an animal. Or simply normal cave sounds, since she wasn't at all sure what those were.

She came to the end of the narrow chute and gently lowered herself until her feet touched solid ground. Winter drew her gun, though she wasn't sure if it'd be safe to fire, since she didn't know how big this space was or what it was made of, other than rock. If she had to fire, the echo of the blast might be enough to give her instant tinnitus. Still, she felt better with the Smith & Wesson pistol in her hand.

"Bryan?" Instead of echoing as she expected, the word was muffled, as if swallowed up by the cavernous space. The flashlight on her jacket illuminated just one chunk of wall at a time, and it all looked the same. White rock and gray shadows. It was so cold, the air constricting her.

Winter had never considered herself claustrophobic per se, but tight spaces were not her favorite. It was at least part of the reason she'd picked an old shoe shop with so many windows as her new office. Being in a fishbowl made her feel safer because at least that way she could see whatever might be coming for her. She could watch her blind spots, stay on her toes. Down here in the dark, she felt vulnerable from every angle.

"It's over, Bryan. The park's surrounded, every exit

blocked off. You'll never get out of here." She turned in a slow circle, examining the walls.

Footsteps rushed by behind her. Winter whirled about, her heart in her throat and her eyes painfully wide. Nothing. She turned the flashlight this way and that, searching.

"Bryan, I know you loved Christina. I'm so sorry about what happened to her. I want you to know that I'm not going to let Nathan get away with it. He deserves to be punished for what he did." She decided to leave out her opinion of the rest of his victims. "And he will be. But you have to give yourself up, Bryan. It's your only chance."

"You lied to me." Bryan's voice seemed to come at her from everywhere at once, ricocheting off the walls, in contrast to hers. She heard one word from here, one from over there. Winter aimed her pistol at the empty walls.

The scuffle of feet came a half a second too late, and she tried to whip around—but the rope caught her around the neck and snapped so tight, it felt like he was taking her head off. The breath was knocked from her lungs, and the blackness in her eyes flashed white.

She lost one sense but kept the others. She felt the cold gravity of the weapon in her hand and the hot force of her assailant behind her. Thinking in a language without words, Winter turned as much as she could, swinging her arm diagonally across her body before pressing the gun into her enemy's flesh. She fired.

Bryan made a choking sound as the rope around her neck went slack.

She snatched it away and began to wheeze, her hand holding her throat as her vision faded back in.

She faced Bryan, weapon still raised and ready to fire. With him dressed all in black with black gloves, she couldn't see the blood. Just a shine of wetness on his gut, on his fingertips. He hadn't lost his footing, not yet.

Her flashlight caught his eyes, turning them yellow. Suddenly, he snatched something from the ground—and rushed her with a wild scream. There was a rock in his hand. He swung his arm back to throw it at her, and she fired into his chest twice more. It was such close range that the impact spun him round, and he fell away from her, face first onto the damp cave floor.

A few seconds passed. She thought she heard voices calling down from above.

"Winter?"

"I'm down here, Noah, in the cave system. There's a rope!" She stepped up to Bryan and crouched at his side. When she pressed her fingertips to his neck, there was nothing.

He was gone.

"Somebody help! Help me, please!" From below, a strangled, weak voice echoed up. A woman's voice.

Aliyah Andry was alive.

45

"Aliyah!" Though Winter had just killed a man, she found herself reeling with another kind of energy. Hope. "Aliyah Andry, this is Winter Black, private investigator. I'm here with the park rangers, police, FBI. We're coming!"

"Thank you! I can't walk! My hip…"

"It's okay. We're coming!"

Noah's voice rang down from above. "Winter, I'm coming down."

"Noah, Aliyah Andry is down here. I'm going to get her. Bryan Green is dead! He's in here too."

"Lyle's calling medevac to the scene, everyone," he shouted.

Winter found another opening not twenty feet from where she'd killed Bryan Green. She could see the night sky above and the lake below.

And Aliyah Andry.

There she was, the moon spotlighting her. She was buried under bushy branches that she was flinging off, one by one. From the look of it, Aliyah must've lost her footing and tumbled down another cliff.

Winter slid down one rock and then the next. It occurred to her that the red glow might've been about Aliyah this whole time, but she'd think about that later.

"Aliyah, I'm coming."

"Thank you, thank you so much. I thought I'd never get out of here." Aliyah started crying.

Winter approached the young woman cautiously. By her flashlight, she could see that there wasn't one square inch of Aliyah's dark skin that wasn't cut or caked with dirt or blood. And her beautiful full lips were cracked and bloody. Winter guessed that was from the ropes more than anything, from the way abrasions stretched across her cheeks.

But Aliyah had fallen next to a lake, and having access to water had saved her life.

Winter knelt to look into her eyes, to really see how she was holding up. Aliyah reached her arms out and hugged her tight, sobbing into her shoulder.

Winter couldn't help but choke on emotion too. "It's okay, Aliyah, it's going to be okay."

The poor woman reeked of sweat and urine and mossy earth, and she was shaking hard. But she wasn't literally freezing. Her skin felt warm. Alive. Which told Winter she really was going to be okay.

"Winter?"

"We're down here." To Aliyah, she said, "He's FBI."

The whir of the helicopter resounded off the walls of the cave. Holding the shaking Aliyah in her arms, Winter listened to its approach.

❄

After the park rangers got Aliyah Andry out, they went in for Bryan Green's body. Noah drove Winter to the hospital to be looked over. The ligature marks around her neck were nasty

—purple bruises, upraised red abrasions. Her voice was hoarse. They'd released her into his care.

She'd woken a few times in the night with coughing fits, and Noah was at her side every moment. Bringing her tepid water, fluffing her pillows, fussing over her. It would've been annoying if it wasn't so cute. But Winter wasn't going to complain. Her neck wound was nothing compared to the torture Aliyah Andry survived at the hands of Bryan Green, not to mention a week in the wilderness.

The young woman was a fighter, and though she'd need physical and emotional therapy to completely heal, Winter felt good about Aliyah's future.

Nathan Lynch had to be airlifted to the hospital. The stab wound in his side had hit his large intestine, causing internal leakage and massive bleeding. He was sent in for surgery the moment he arrived and spent the night in critical condition. That morning, she'd received a call from Deputy Mullaney updating her on his condition.

Bryan Green had been crueler to Nathan Lynch than any of the others. And that was saying something.

He'd been beaten to the point of unconsciousness at least once, if not several times. His nose was broken, his cheekbone fractured, and two of his teeth were so loose that he was going to need implants. Bryan had configured his ropes in such a way that sharp knots dug into Nathan's skin all over his body, leaving him with nasty bruises, abrasions, and even some puncture wounds.

"Like a dalmatian." Mullaney's words echoed in her head.

And Lynch's feet were shattered. Apparently, Bryan had stuck them under the wheel of his Jeep and run them over several times. And his feet hadn't been flat on the ground. They were lashed together and stacked, so the bones pressed into each other when they shattered.

He'd need significant reconstructive surgery if he was

ever going to walk on them again, and he'd probably need to wear braces the rest of his life. His climbing days were at an end.

But those were only the beginning of Nathan Lynch's problems.

While he languished in the hospital, the Austin PD would be building and filing their case against him. All the damning evidence that had been left out for them, stacked in neat little piles because Bryan Green had interrupted Nathan's evidence-shredding party.

Nathan was about to be fired from his job and arrested. He was getting divorced. His cushy, playboy life as he knew it was over.

46

Winter slept in late the next morning. She had a vague memory of Noah kissing her forehead while she was still asleep and telling her that he'd been called into the office.

She awoke to an empty house. With no desire to expend any effort to do anything, she ordered in her morning mocha latte and sat on the front porch drinking it and just looking at the street and the sky. She knew there might be a camera attached to a telephone pole or something. That even though Carl Gardner was dead, somebody might be watching her. Still, she couldn't bring herself to give a shit. Not today.

Watch away, asshole. I hope you like my ratty-ass bathrobe.

Just as she tucked one leg under the other to get even cozier, she saw Beulah rounding the corner toward their home.

She set her coffee down and stood as Noah stepped out of the truck, searching for his expression. When he turned to face her, his eyes were soft and there was a peaceful smile on his lips.

She still had no idea what had happened—if he was still a

part of the FBI or not. Either way, whatever had made him smile like that had to be a good thing.

"A one-year sabbatical, paid at one-third my usual rate." He stepped onto the porch and gave her a soft kiss.

Winter smiled up at him. She couldn't remember the last time she'd seen him so relaxed. It was like a two-thousand-pound weight had been lifted from his shoulders.

She might have to pick up some extra jobs to take care of the slack, but she had every confidence Noah would help out with that. Finally, he'd have a chance to recharge his battery and focus on their own problems without constantly feeling guilty.

They sat back down on the porch, and he hooked an arm around her.

"I bet Eve's disappointed." She fiddled with one of the buttons on his shirt. "Do you think they'll get her a new partner?"

He shrugged and stretched his shoulders. "I dunno. I'd be kinda sad to be replaced, but I'd also be sad thinking of her spending the next year all alone in that windowless office with nothing but Pokey and Pokette for company."

Winter suppressed a shiver. After the incident with Bryan Green, she was convinced she'd rather be submitted to dental torture than have to work in an office without windows.

Her phone rang. She didn't recognize the number.

"Where's the two-fifteen area code?"

Noah groaned as he thought. "Shit, I know this. Boston?"

"I don't think so. But it is familiar." She swiped to answer. "Hello?"

"Hello, might I speak with Winter Black, please?" The voice was male, gravelly, and unfamiliar.

"Speaking."

"Hello, Ms. Black. My name is Detective Gilbert Clemont

with the Philadelphia Police Department, Eighth District. How are you doing today?"

"Hi. I'm…fine."

"I'm afraid I have some bad news about a family member of yours, Opal Drewitt. She was found dead in her car this morning."

"What?" Winter sat up like a shot. "What happened?"

"We're working on that, ma'am. She had multiple stab wounds, but nothing was taken from the scene, including her wallet, which had over five hundred dollars cash inside."

Noah set his hand lightly on the small of Winter's back. "What's going on?"

"Opal's dead…" Winter's mouth hung slack, twitching over the words. With everything that had been happening with Kline and Gardner and Justin's fans, it seemed like one hell of a coincidence.

Had Justin's fans killed Opal? They'd used her to help find Winter, manipulated her kindness, and then exterminated her like a rodent.

And then it hit her. Kline had been there, visiting with his sister.

Winter's heart dropped like a stone through wet tissue. "Is her broth…her friend around? A man named Kline Hurst around? Is he okay?"

"He's here with me. We found him at her home. But he's going to have to stay in Philly 'til we can verify his alibi."

Winter knew that was standard, but the words still left her vibrating with anger. "Kline would never hurt Opal. They've been…close since childhood."

"Yes, that's what he said as well. But we can't be too careful with these things."

"Can I speak to him? You said he's there with you…"

"Sure." His voice faded and she heard him say, "She wants to speak to you."

A moment and a few scratchy sounds later, his voice came on the line. It echoed slightly as if on speaker phone. "Winter?"

"Kline? Oh, my god, are you okay?"

"I'm fine. Don't worry. I'll be back in Austin before you know it."

"I'm so sorry about Opal."

The echo of the speaker phone shut off, and the detective's voice returned. "I'll remind him to give you a call when we're finished with questioning."

"Okay. Thank you." They hung up, and Winter dropped the phone limply into her lap. "Somebody killed Opal. Stabbed her to death."

"Oh, shit." Noah's head dropped.

"It's Justin, isn't it? His sick followers out there fucking with me and my family." Winter jumped to her feet, rage edging out her sadness. "They're hunting us like trophies."

"You don't know that. It could be—"

"I do know that!" She turned on him. "And you know that. Somebody killed her and didn't steal anything, left hundreds of dollars in her wallet. Who else would kill Opal?"

My aunt.

"We don't know her. We don't know who else might kill her."

"It's too close to Justin, too much of a coincidence. I don't buy it. They killed Opal to prove to me what they're made of. To show me that no matter what I do, I'll never be safe." She wrapped her arms around herself, as if to hold in her anger. "It's exactly what Justin would do in this situation."

Noah didn't argue with her. He shook with frustration and scratched at his neck. "I did see this unfamiliar home on Gardner's computer. It was pricey. One of those big-ass places built in the woods somewhere, cameras in all the rooms with tall-ass ceilings. It didn't strike me as the kind of place that Kline or his sister would have. 'Course, we don't know his sister."

"True, but it's not what I imagined for her either."

"And we don't really know Kline."

Winter side-eyed him.

"What he did was illegal, if he's even telling the truth about it."

Before Winter could defend the father she'd just learned she had, her phone dinged with a text message. She whipped it open, hoping it would be something from Kline explaining what had happened. Instead, she found herself gazing down at a restricted number.

Every family has its secrets, the message read. *But you can't keep secrets from me.*

The End
To be continued...

Thank you for reading.
All of the Winter Black Series books can be found on Amazon.

ACKNOWLEDGMENTS

The past few years have been a whirlwind of change, both personally and professionally, and I find myself at a loss for the right words to express my profound gratitude to those who have supported me on this remarkable journey. Yet, I am compelled to try.

To my sons, whose unwavering support has been my bedrock, granting me the time and energy to transform my darkest thoughts into words on paper. Your steadfast belief in me has never faltered, and watching each of you grow, welcoming the wonderful daughters you've brought into our family, has been a source of immense pride and joy.

Embarking on the dual role of both author and publisher has been an exhilarating, albeit challenging, adventure. Transitioning from the solitude of writing to the dynamic world of publishing has opened new horizons for me, and I'm deeply grateful for the opportunity to share my work directly with you, the readers.

I extend my heartfelt thanks to the entire team at Mary Stone Publishing, the same dedicated group who first recognized my potential as an indie author years ago. Your collective efforts, from the editors whose skillful hands have polished my words to the designers, marketers, and support staff who breathe life into these books, have been instrumental in resonating deeply with our readers. Each of you plays a crucial role in this journey, not only nurturing my growth but also ensuring that every story reaches its full potential. Your dedication, creativity, and finesse have been nothing short of invaluable.

However, my deepest gratitude is reserved for you, my beloved readers. You ventured off the beaten path of traditional publishing to embrace my work, investing your most precious asset—your time. It is my sincerest hope that this book has enriched that time, leaving you with memories that linger long after the last page is turned.

With all my love and heartfelt appreciation,

Mary

ABOUT THE AUTHOR

Nestled in the serene Blue Ridge Mountains of East Tennessee, Mary Stone crafts her stories surrounded by the natural beauty that inspires her. What was once a home filled with the lively energy of her sons has now become a peaceful writer's retreat, shared with cherished pets and the vivid characters of her imagination.

As her sons grew and welcomed wonderful daughters-in-law into the family, Mary's life entered a quieter phase, rich with opportunities for deep creative focus. In this tranquil environment, she weaves tales of courage, resilience, and intrigue, each story a testament to her evolving journey as a writer.

From childhood fears of shadowy figures under the bed to a profound understanding of humanity's real-life villains, Mary's style has been shaped by the realization that the most complex antagonists often hide in plain sight. Her writing is characterized by strong, multifaceted heroines who defy traditional roles, standing as equals among their peers in a world of suspense and danger.

Mary's career has blossomed from being a solitary author to establishing her own publishing house—a significant milestone that marks her growth in the literary world. This expansion is not just a personal achievement but a reflection of her commitment to bring thrilling and thought-provoking stories to a wider audience. As an author and publisher, Mary continues to challenge the conventions of the thriller genre, inviting readers into gripping tales filled with serial killers, astute FBI agents, and intrepid heroines who confront peril with unflinching bravery.

Each new story from Mary's pen—or her publishing house—is a pledge to captivate, thrill, and inspire, continuing the legacy of the imaginative little girl who once found wonder and mystery in the shadows.

Discover more about Mary Stone on her website.
www.authormarystone.com

- facebook.com/authormarystone
- x.com/MaryStoneAuthor
- goodreads.com/AuthorMaryStone
- bookbub.com/profile/3378576590
- pinterest.com/MaryStoneAuthor
- instagram.com/marystoneauthor
- tiktok.com/@authormarystone

Printed in Great Britain
by Amazon